Travis arrived at my door wearing gray khakis, looking as casual as a member of the establishment could. Where was the artist I had met in the park?

If only we weren't going to Tanya's house. That was the downer. "Does Tanya know you invited me?" I asked when we were in his car.

"No. She said we could bring guests. You're my guest."

"Will it be a big party?"

"Depends upon how many guests the main guests invite."

"Main guests?"

"The class officers."

"Oh, that's right."

"Are you in the spirit of this, or are you somewhere else?"

"In the spirit "

"Great."

At Tanya's house I walked hesitantly up the front steps with Travis. But as he rang the doorbell, I had the happy thought that Tanya would be unpleasantly shocked to see me with Travis. He was considered such a catch at school. Maybe she was even trying to catch him herself. My spirits lifted considerably as the door opened, and fell considerably when I saw Matt Green standing there.

MARJORIE SHARMAT has written many well-known books for young adults, including *Square Pegs, I Saw Him First, How to Meet a Gorgeous Girl, How to Meet a Gorgeous Guy, How to Have a Gorgeous Wedding,* and *He Noticed I'm Alive . . . and Other Hopeful Signs,* all available in Dell Laurel-Leaf editions. She lives in Tucson, Arizona.

Two Guys Noticed Me...
AND OTHER MIRACLES

A NOVEL BY
**MARJORIE
SHARMAT**

LAUREL-LEAF BOOKS

LAUREL-LEAF BOOKS bring together under a single imprint outstanding works of fiction and nonfiction particularly suitable for young adult readers, both in and out of the classroom. Charles F. Reasoner, Professor Emeritus of Children's Literature and Reading, New York University, is consultant to this series.

Published by
Dell Publishing Co., Inc.
1 Dag Hammarskjold Plaza
New York, New York 10017

Laurel-Leaf Library ® TM 766734, Dell Publishing Co., Inc.

ISBN: 0-440-98846-2

RL: 5.8

Reprinted by arrangement with Delacorte Press

Printed in the United States of America

December 1986

10 9 8 7 6 5 4 3 2 1

WFH

Two Guys Noticed Me...

AND OTHER MIRACLES

1

I fell in love forever this past summer. At least that's the way it seemed to me. His name was Matt Green. On the first day of my vacation from school, he showed up at my front door with his mother, Gossamer Green. My father had invited them for dinner. My mother had walked out on my father and me and our beautiful home in the suburbs of New York City two years earlier, so it was certainly okay for my father to invite a woman for dinner. And who was I to complain if she had a tall handsome son? I fell for Matt and Matt fell for me. I think that was the order in which it happened, although I like to think it was simultaneous.

If my life had proceeded smoothly from summer into fall, I would never have questioned my feelings about Matt. But fall went haywire. It started when my mother, after two years of traveling around the world, decided to come home. It wasn't a particularly convenient time, since my father had just about decided to marry Gossamer Green and was busy trying to divorce my mother. My mother had walked out on us in order to find herself. She had sent cheery postcards to us along the way. I didn't think it was right that she had a good time finding herself after deserting us.

One afternoon, a week after school resumed, a taxi pulled up in front of my house. I was home alone. Betty, our part-time maid, was off, and my father was at work in his law firm in the city. I saw a woman getting out of the taxi. The driver helped her with her five suitcases. I was watching from a front window. I had been looking out the window on and off for days. My mother had written that she'd be coming back sometime this week.

There she was! I didn't recognize the clothes she was wearing, but I recognized her. Suddenly I wasn't motherless anymore. I was a valid, authentic daughter with both a mother and a father. But I was shaking. As I watched her climb the front stairs, I could feel it. Why should *I* shake? I hadn't deserted anyone. I felt resentment and love. I wished my father were home. I needed someone to tell me how to act toward my mother.

I went to the door. But my mother opened it before I got there. No knocking, no ringing of the doorbell. That told me something. She felt this was still *her* house.

"Jody!" she said in a soft voice. She grabbed me and

hugged me. The hug must have lasted five minutes. It was like putting something cold into the oven and waiting for it to warm up. But I couldn't warm up.

My mother stepped back so she could look me over. I knew I had changed. I was thirteen when she left home. I get tired of people telling me I'm a young lady now, so fortunately she didn't say that. She just said, "It's wonderful to be back with you."

Close up I could see that my mother had grown a little older. Nothing significant. People who liked my mother always used to say she was pretty. The others used to say she was looking well.

There we were. My mother, me, five suitcases, and the kind of embarrassment that should never happen between a mother and a daughter.

"Let's sit down," I said finally. We went into the living room, which is the room you invite strangers into. My mother sat down in the gold-on-gold-striped velvet easy chair that she had purchased shortly before she skipped out. She took off her shoes and started to talk. "Well, Jody, I'm back. I'm *sorry* I had to leave you and your father, but when I left I truly didn't know who I was. Now I know."

"*Who?*"

My mother smoothed her hair. She had a new hairdo, kind of sleek and short. It made her eyes look bigger. "Jody," she said, "it's not that simple. I'm talking about layers and layers of identity. Of self-knowledge."

"I know who I am and I never bothered with that identity stuff. If you don't bother with that stuff, you just automatically know who you are. Mom, it isn't a reason for leaving home."

My mother smoothed her hair again. Then she frowned. "Please, Jody, you'll see that I'm a new person."

"They teach you how to become a new person at the community college on Monday and Wednesday nights. There's a course with a name like that . . . something about the new you. You didn't have to travel around the world and leave Dad and me. You could have gone to the community college on Monday and Wednesday nights."

My mother kept frowning. Now I remembered that frown from years ago. "Jody, you're too young to understand what I mean. So let's just stop talking about my traveling and try to catch up on the two years we've lost. Is Alison August still your best friend? Do you have any boyfriends? Are you still getting good marks at school? You're a junior now, aren't you?"

"Mom, I can't prepare a summary for you. This isn't a class reunion. Stick around and you'll find out everything. I can't give you back the two years by summing them up."

"She's right, Sue."

My father was standing there! He had slipped into the house. He was home early either by chance or because he somehow knew that this was *the* day.

My mother got up from her chair. "Gerald!" she said.

"Hello, Sue."

They both sort of partially extended a hand and then let the hand hang and then withdrew it. I was glad to see that I wasn't the only one who didn't know how to act in this situation.

I was in the way. I had to clear out and let them be alone. "I'm going to do some sketching," I said. "See you guys later."

"Sketching?" said my mother. "You're still at that? Fine. We'll have to talk and talk about sketching."

I practically bolted from the house with my sketch-book and pencil. Then I wondered, what if my mother left again while I was out? What if she left and *never* came back? Why hadn't I been nicer to her? It was all those excuses she was making for leaving us. I didn't buy them.

I kept on walking. I walked to the park. Sometimes I sketch there. I sat down on a bench. I didn't feel like sketching. I was dying to know what was going on back at the house between my mother and father. Would he kick her out? Could he kick her out? My father was a lawyer, the correct kind who always meticulously avoids showing any skin between the top of his expensive dark ribbed stockings and the bottom of his expensively tailored trousers. He also regularly contributes a hefty sum to the United Way. He was not inclined to kick a wife out into the cold world. He might, however, negotiate her out, utiliz-ing the vast legal resources of Winkleman, Hackett, Lipsert, Ives, Kline & Bradford. My father, Gerald Kline, whose name was securely nestled between

Ives and Bradford in the firm's title, would never scratch, kick, or bite.

I looked around the park. It was crowded. But there was only one other artist there. It was a guy, sitting on the ground with his back toward me. He was wearing a woolen plaid jacket, the kind that disguises whether you're fat, thin, or simply in need of warmth. He was painting a picture of a horse. There were no horses around, so he had to be doing it from memory. I stood up and walked over to him. He didn't notice me standing behind him. I studied his picture. It was wonderful.

"You have a great eye for composition," I said. "The way that horse is standing in front of the fence, the way the fence is placed so that it could be a barrier or could be . . ." I stopped. I was probably interrupting his concentration. He nodded but he didn't turn around. I kept standing there like an idiot anyway. Maybe I was looking for another artistic soul. Art is my passion. Someday I'm going to be a professional. My favorite portrait so far is the one I did of Matt.

"You're breathing over my shoulder," the guy said, still not turning around.

"Is there a law?" I started to walk away.

"Come back," he said. He still didn't turn around.

"I'm leaving to find myself," I said.

Why did I say that? I must have had my mother on my brain. Out of the blue, it sounded crazy.

"I'm rude when I paint," he said. "Sorry."

I guess we both turned at the same time. He stood

up. We faced each other. I had expected him to have a sunken look, and a wan, aesthetic expression, like a proper artist. Artistic talent demands sacrifices. You can't paint and try out for the football team. No way. Then again, as he faced me, I realized that there are exceptions. I don't know much about football, but he looked like a tackle or a guard or whoever does the killing for the team.

2

Maybe I looked like *I* did the killing for the football team. I was upset over my mother's return, and my father's reaction to my mother, and my own reaction to my mother. I needed someone warm and friendly, not this guy who started out rude and then thought he could simply apologize for it.

He was wearing glasses, which made him look more macho. Sometimes glasses work the other way.

"What's your name?" he asked.

"Jody. Jody Kline. What's yours?"

"Pablo. Pablo Picasso."

"Right."

"You don't believe me?"

"Sure I believe you. What's not to believe?"

"Don't you know me?"

He asked the question seriously. I kept looking at him. He looked familiar.

I answered, "Of course I know you, Mr. Picasso."

"I also have another name."

"No kidding."

He hesitated. "My other name's T. C."

"Really? That's one of my favorite names."

He smiled. "Should we start this conversation all over again?"

"No, I just wanted you to know that I like your picture."

"Are you an artist? Is that a sketchbook you're carrying?"

I looked down at my sketchbook, as if to check on what I was carrying. It was a silly thing to do. But there was something about this guy that caught me off guard.

"Yes," I said. "Sometimes I sketch in the park. But today I've gone blank."

"I know the feeling. I paint here now and then. But I've never seen you here before. Do you come at a special time?"

"Not really. And now with the weather turning cool, and school starting, I'll probably give it up until the spring. Uh, can I ask you a question?"

"Why am I painting a horse in the park when there isn't any horse?" He smiled at me. "Is that the question?"

"Something like that," I answered.

"This park makes me feel like a painter. Sometimes I actually do paint the trees, the benches, the people."

"Are you going to be a painter when you—"

"When I grow up? Yes and no. I'm planning to be an architect. But I'll continue to paint. And if my paintings sell, good-bye architecture." T. C. looked at his watch. "And speaking of good-bye, I have to go home. Maybe I'll see you here again."

"Maybe."

I walked off. I didn't want just to stand there while he packed up to leave. I wanted him to ask me some questions about myself, but he didn't. I wanted him to ask me when I'd be coming back to the park, but he didn't. I shouldn't have cared what he did or didn't do. I had Matt.

I went back to the bench and sat there for at least an hour. It was getting dark. Time to go home. Would my mother still be there? I hoped I wouldn't come in on a fight between my mother and father.

I got up and walked home. My parents had left the living room. They were sitting, very civilized, in the kitchen, drinking tea and eating brownies! Unreal.

My mother beckoned me to sit down. The memory of all the times the three of us had sat around the kitchen table came back. It's strange how the mind stores these pictures, ready to be recalled or buried forever.

I sat down. My mother said, "Jody, the three of us are in an awkward situation. I realize that it's going to take time for your father and you to adjust to my being home. You probably know that your father initiated divorce proceedings while I was away. I understand. But now that I'm back, I'd like to sweep all of that under the rug and start anew."

My mother seemed confident. Full of hope. Maybe she was euphoric from the tea and brownies.

I looked at my father. He was wearing his expressionless lawyer expression, which takes in information but is careful not to send anything out.

My mother continued. "I'm moving back into the house. I'll be staying in the guest room for a while. We're going to let this situation evolve rather than force it to be right."

Force it to be right! Would it ever be right? Did my father tell my mother he was planning to marry Gossamer Green? He should tell my mother. Right away. My mother had been unfair to my father, and now I was afraid that my father was being unfair to my mother.

My mother stood up. "I'm going to unpack," she said. "After I've settled in, we'll have a nice long talk, Jody. I love you." She bent over and kissed my forehead. Then she swept out of the room. My mother has a flair for sweeping out of rooms, like a movie star making an exit.

The moment she was out of sight, I turned to my father. "Did you tell her about Gossamer?"

"Not yet."

"Not *yet? When?*"

"Soon. She just walked in. I can't hit her with it."

"Are you having second thoughts about Gossamer?"

"No. I'm just in shock. Your mother's here, in the flesh. It's so difficult to absorb."

"Dad, remember when I told Alison a lie and I

wanted to postpone telling her the truth? You asked me if I was familiar with the expression 'now or never.' You said it had merit. Remember? You made me call Alison and confess. I did and she got mad at me. But we made up. I might still have that hanging over me if you hadn't made me take care of it."

"This is different, Jody."

"No, it really isn't. You're kind of living a lie by planning to marry Gossamer and not telling Mom about it. That's worse than telling a lie, isn't it?"

I was sorry I asked. My father, being a lawyer, can always come up with a convoluted answer to a simple question. But this time he didn't. "I'll know when the time is right," he said.

I wondered if my father still loved my mother. Maybe that was it. Maybe he wasn't sure anymore that he wanted to marry Gossamer. That moment when he sort of extended his hand to my mother and then didn't seem to know what to do, could he have been falling back in love with her? It could have hit him like it hit me the moment I met Matt. Then again, it could have hit him like an ulcer attack, unwanted but undeniable. I was in the middle of a sticky mess. If my father dumped Gossamer, what would happen to Matt and me? Would Matt hate the Kline family?

Tonight, for the first time in two years, my mother, my father, and I would all be sleeping under the same roof. I should have felt serene and happy, but instead it seemed to me that our family was on the verge of an explosion.

3

Alison August and I walked to school together the next day. We often walk to school together. Alison is a junior like me. She knows about my family situation, but she's not advertising it. Except to her boyfriend, Pete Summers. Alison advertises almost everything to him. She can't help it.

"So how does she look?" Alison asked as we walked along. "And how does she act? And how does your father act? And is it all an act?"

"Well, they're polite to each other."

"Sounds deadly."

"Yeah, well . . . hey, is that him?"

"Who?" Alison was looking around.

"T. C. A guy I met at the park yesterday. An artist. I think that's him across the street. I recognize the jacket. Wait a minute. I *know* him. Yesterday he was wearing glasses and he was hunched over a canvas part of the time and he was T. C. Today he's—"

"You *met* him?" said Alison. "Travis Cameo. He wears glasses? Half of the girls in school have a crush on him. He's vice-president of the senior class."

"I know it. But it didn't connect yesterday. When I met him in the park, I didn't think about him as a guy from school. I've probably passed him in the halls over and over."

"What's he like? I mean, what's he really like? I've heard he's conceited. Is he?"

"I only spoke to him for a few minutes. And he was rude in the beginning. But he's a wonderful painter. Hey, Travis!"

I have no idea why I called his name. It wasn't like me. It was like me to observe and analyze, but not to yell to a guy across the street. He turned. He stopped. He waved. Then he walked on.

"Well, the great one had a wave for you. That's something," said Alison. "Anyway, you should care. You have Matt. You don't care, do you? You're not attracted to Travis, are you?"

"Of course not!"

"You answered awfully fast," said Alison. "Just watch your step. He's got so many admirers you could trip over them."

"Well, I'm not one of them. What's to admire, except his paintings?"

Alison looked astonished. "You're kidding, of course. If I weren't madly in love with Pete, which I am . . ." Alison stopped talking. She nudged me. "Brace yourself. Look who's coming toward us."

Tanya Lipsert, daughter of one of my father's law partners, walked up to us. I didn't like Tanya. She had a lovely mother and her father was okay, but Tanya was a weasel. The more I knew her, the more I thought she was a weasel. And she had a thing for Matt. When Matt first asked me out, I had to break the date due to circumstances beyond my control that I don't want to think about. Matt ended up going out with Tanya via a blind date arranged by her father. That was the first and last time they went out together, but I knew she cared for him. Matt spent the summer working at Winkleman, Hackett, Lipsert, Ives, Kline & Bradford, and Tanya made a point of trying to see Matt whenever she visited her father at the firm. My father reported this to me. Now Matt was a student at Columbia University, and he worked only part time for the law firm. Tanya visited the firm less often, but on a relentlessly accurate schedule. She never missed Matt.

All these things were going through my mind as Tanya approached. She had never liked me, but because of Matt, she liked me even less. She was absolutely beaming. "Jody, congratulations! I hear that you've got your mother back!"

Tanya was in good form. She was *congratulating* me on the return of my mother. I'd love to slap her across the face. I try to be civil to her because of our fathers' connection. I was stuck with her.

Alison, however, was not stuck with Tanya. *"Congratulations* is a stupid word, Tanya."

"Why? Under the circumstances I think it's a real *achievement* that your mother came back, Jody."

"It's an achievement that your parents allow you in their house," said Alison. "You must have fooled them into thinking that you're a real human being. How do you manage that anyway?"

Tanya walked away.

"Thanks," I said to Alison.

"My pleasure. But how did she know that your mother's back?"

"My father must have told her father. I wish he hadn't done that. I haven't told Matt yet. I told him that my mother was coming home. But now my mother's back in our house, under our roof, and I don't think Gossamer or Matt know about it. I'm going to call Matt after school."

"Sticky. His mother is planning to marry your father. Your mother's back in the house. Excuse me if I'm overstepping, but for someone who makes a living advising people, your father could use some advice himself. I can't understand people who can't make up their minds about love. I know I love Pete and he loves me. It's so easy."

For Alison, it was too easy. That's just my opinion, of course. She had never, ever looked at another guy. I wasn't terribly fond of Pete Summers. I thought Alison deserved better, but Alison didn't think better existed.

The school day passed quickly. I saw Travis in the

cafeteria. He saw me, too, but he didn't come over. After school I walked home by myself. I went a little out of my way and passed through the park. Why did I do that? Travis had been so aloof. Did that make me want to see him again? He wasn't in the park. I walked on to my house.

As I neared my house, I saw a gray-blue sports car parked in front of it. Maybe my mother had a new car. I went up the front steps. This was the first time in two years that I'd be coming home from school and finding my mother there. I opened the front door and stepped inside. My mother was there, all right, and there was a man with her.

4

They were sitting on the couch in the living room. My mother was wearing a simple sweater and skirt. My mother felt she looked her best in a simple sweater and skirt, so this meant she cared how she looked for this man.

The man. He was introduced as Uncle Mike. My mother said the name slowly and carefully. There was no mistake about it. He was Uncle Mike. A name like that, attached to a grown man you find sitting on your living room couch, requires some kind of explanation. My mother explained: "Uncle Mike owns a chain of fitness camps for children and adults. He's always been known as Uncle Mike, and now there are dozens of Uncle Mike fitness franchises opening up. Isn't that right, Uncle Mike?"

My mother seemed to have gotten her information from Uncle Mike, and like a kid afraid to make a mistake on a test, she was rechecking her facts with teacher. Uncle Mike was basking in the recital of his successes. He was huge and towering, even though he was sitting relaxed on the sofa. Dressed in a jacket, shirt, tie, neat pants, crew socks, and blazing white sneakers, he projected a split image of responsible businessman and manic sportsman. I got the impression that he was wealthy. Success allows you to be strange and quaint. But where had my mother found him? She could tell I was puzzled.

"Jody," she said, "I met Uncle Mike in London a couple of months ago when he was on a business trip. We've kept in touch."

"What your mother means," said Uncle Mike with a smile, "is that I've kept in touch with her. She said she was planning to return to the States. Well, my main offices are in New York City, and when your mother came home I just popped right out here to welcome her back."

He popped right out. Instantly! My mother had just returned yesterday. What kind of relationship was this anyway? This guy was no joke. From all reports, at least from my mother's report, Uncle Mike was a super-successful businessman.

He stood up. Loomed up, I should say. "Time to be getting back," he said.

"Won't you reconsider and stay for dinner?" my mother asked.

She wanted my father to meet Uncle Mike. That had to be it!

"Love to, but business awaits. And so does my

apartment. Why did I move into a penthouse in a skyscraper? Gorgeous view, but ill-designed."

Uncle Mike walked toward the door. He turned to me. "I'll be seeing you again soon, I hope."

"Sure."

My mother opened the door for Uncle Mike. "I'll call you in a couple of days, Sue," he said.

My mother nodded. Uncle Mike left. At least there wasn't any kissy-kissy business. Maybe I cramped their style.

My mother was humming.

"Mom, what was that all about? Who is that guy?"

"Just a friend."

"A special friend?"

"What do you mean?"

"You know. If he's a special friend, why did you move back into the house? Are you trying to make Dad jealous? Is this a game?"

"Your father's going to marry Gossamer Green."

"You *know?*"

"Your father told me last night. We had a long, quiet, rather dreary talk."

"Are you moving out?"

"No. Never. He can move out when he marries her. This is my house. You're my daughter."

"So what are *you* going to do? Marry Uncle Mike?"

My mother laughed. "And become Aunt Sue, Queen of the Uncle Mike Fitness Camps? No, thanks. He's just a friend. Good company, powerful, rich, but just a pal."

"You think Dad will be jealous of him."

"Jody!"

"It's true. He contacted you as soon as you got back home, and you let him."

"Because I need a friend to talk to, and he has good advice. And quite frankly, I need someone who *accepts* me. Jody, I haven't shared anything with you yet. Let me tell you about my travels, my discoveries."

"I just met one of your discoveries."

"Please, Jody."

"Later, Mom. Okay? I have a phone call to make."

"Is it a boy?"

"I'm calling Matt Green, Gossamer's son. He's my boyfriend, Mom."

She had to find out some time.

"Well, now, *that's* a cozy situation. Looks like the Greens have taken over my family lock, stock, and barrel."

"Matt's terrific. He just entered Columbia, and he works part time in Dad's office."

"Cozier and cozier. I feel so left out."

"Don't feel that way. You'll like Matt."

"I'm looking forward to meeting him."

I wasn't looking forward to the meeting. But at least she knew how things stood. My father had told my mother about Gossamer. He'd taken *my* advice. I was coming up in the world.

I went to my room. I called Matt at the law office. "My mother's home," I said. "In case you didn't know."

"I know she's home," he said. There was a harsh edge to his voice.

I hesitated. "Are we still going to see each other this weekend?"

"Sure. I have to study one day. But I have an idea for a super Saturday or a super Sunday. Choose one."

"I guess I'll study Saturday and reward myself Sunday. I choose super Sunday."

I hoped it would be. I didn't like the way he'd said, "I know she's home."

5

My mother desperately wanted to do something "mother-daughter." She said, "Let's go shopping." "Want to visit the art gallery?" "How about trying that new French restaurant?" Finally she descended to my level and said, "You know that secondhand shop you liked so much? The one with the odor of burning incense and all the salespeople in exhumed clothes? Let's spend a fun hour there."

"I don't think so, Mom."

I wasn't playing hard to get. Every time I looked at my mother, I realized she was my one and only mother, that her place in my life was unique, that she was basically a decent person, and that flightiness and a trendy kind of selfishness shouldn't earn her a lifetime demerit. Besides, I was already thirteen when she left home. The simple shared ordinariness of living under the same roof with her all those thirteen years made us mother and daughter forever.

But when she left, she damaged the relationship. Now she was working like crazy to repair it. But I was too old to be enticed and seduced. "Mom," I said, "I'm not into exhumed clothes anymore. I never really was. Alison heard a rumor that certain stores accepted clothes that briefly spent time on corpses, so we used to go into used-clothing stores and ask to see corpse-worn outfits. It was our idea of a joke."

"So you outgrew it? Splendid. What are you into now?"

"I just do normal things. Go to school, draw, paint, go to horror movies—"

"Horror movies? That's new. I don't recall your going to horror movies. I suppose it's not as morbid as corpse-clothes."

"All the kids go to horror movies. Look, someday soon we'll go to that French restaurant, okay?"

"No, I'd rather do *your* kind of thing with you. The horror scene. I'll share that with you."

She won. It was Saturday night and I had been studying all day. I was looking forward to seeing Matt the next day, and I had spent Saturday earning it. My mother knew that I was finally finished with my studying. I was free to share a delicious night of horror.

As we stood in the long line outside the movie theater, my mother asked, "Is this 'PG' or 'R' or 'X' or whatever you kids have to watch out for?"

I shrugged. "You picked out the movie."

"Because I knew you'd like it, Jody."

I looked at the line. I seemed to be the only mother-accompanied person. Way in back of us I recognized Amy Vincetti and Linda Johnson. Amy came up to me when she saw me, while Linda kept her place for her in line.

"Hi, Amy," I said. "I'd like you to meet my mother."

"Your *mother?*"

I guess the word hadn't completely gotten around school that my mother was back.

My mother smiled. "I've returned from my trip."

Amy squirmed. Then she said, "We're all happy to have you back."

Amy returned to her place in line with great haste.

"I guess the whole school knows I was gone," said my mother.

"Well, a few kids here and there . . ."

"A full-blown curiosity, that's what I am."

"For about five minutes. The kids are more interested in, uh, computers, romance, clothes, world affairs . . ."

"I'm not complaining. It's fun to be out with my daughter and her friends on a Saturday night."

It wasn't fun for my mother's daughter. It looks odd to go to the movies with your mother on a Saturday night. Maybe my friends thought she came back in order to guard me permanently.

My mother bought popcorn for me, herself, Amy, and Linda. She was everybody's chum. The movie was gross. But my mother said she was pleased to see an all-American film again. So we watched all-American humanoids up there, shedding their scaly blue skin.

After the movie my mother rounded up Amy and Linda and took all of us to a pizzeria. She definitely wanted to be part of the action. I knew this for certain when she waved to four guys in the next booth. Then she motioned for them to come over. I froze. One of the guys was Travis Cameo! And here I was on a Saturday night with my mother.

The boys shrugged, looked at one another, stood up, and came over. Then they stood over the four of us in our booth. They hadn't the vaguest idea what to do next. Travis nodded to me as if he recognized me. But I was no longer an artistic sylvan nymph materializing in the park, but rather the prized offering of an aggressive mother in a pizza parlor.

I knew the other three boys slightly. One of them was Duane Rabinowitz, who goes after anything wearing a skirt. He would not be reluctant to go after my mother.

"We've just seen *Humanoids, Future Family Next Door*," my mother said. "Seen it?"

One of the boys chuckled. "Naw, we passed. We already got freaky next-door neighbors."

Amy and Linda giggled.

"Sit down and join us," said my mother. "Pizza's on me tonight."

There was no room to sit down. The booth was only big enough to seat four people. Four of us were already sitting in it.

"Guess we'll have to break up," said my mother. "Why don't we do this: boy, girl, boy, girl, boy, girl, boy, girl." My mother stood up and touched my arm. "If you and I go to the next booth and two of the young men take our places here and the other two go to the next booth with us, it will work."

Amy looked pleased. Linda looked bewildered. Mrs. Gerald Kline was getting them dates and paying for their pizzas. It was an unexpected and confusing bounty. The whole strange situation was rounded off by an opportunistic Duane asking if my mother would pay for both anchovies *and* mushrooms.

My mother and I slid into the booth formerly occupied by the four guys. She was opposite me, in keeping with her boy-girl-boy-girl plan. In the other booth the two girls were opposite the two boys. My mother's experience in arranging seating for fancy dinner parties at our home didn't quite work in a pizza booth. Travis sat down beside me, and Duane sat down next to my mother. My mother and I were double-dating!

I should have gone to that French restaurant with her, dined on some kind of sour-tasting duck, spent a couple of hours in that elegant world, and satisfied my mother's mother-daughter togetherness yearnings. Now my mother was sitting next to the class letch, and Travis was sitting next to a girl who was so hard up her mother had to get and pay for her dates. At least that's the impression I would have gotten if I were Travis. He hardly said a word. I suppose I could have been flattered that he decided to sit in my booth. But curiosity of the type that the Pied Piper thrived on probably got the best of him.

The eight of us ordered. The boys had probably arrived at the pizzeria shortly before we did, because no one had been eating. Now some of the kids seemed reluctant to order as much as they wanted because my mother was paying. But some of the kids were inspired to order more. A student of human behavior would have had a field day studying the reactions.

I was so aware of Travis sitting beside me that it was hard to dig into the food when it came. He was hunched over in a way that looks great on rugged guys and terrible on anyone else. He turned and talked to me. "Been back to the park lately?"

"Not really. Sometimes I walk through."

Subconsciously looking for you, I was thinking.

"Have you been back?" I asked.

"One time. I finished my horse."

"How did it come out?"

"Okay."

My mother would have been interested in this conversation, but she had her own diversion. Duane Rabinowitz was giving her the eye. Pretty soon he would be giving her the knee. Duane's lust knew no age limits. He thrived on all the good things in life: crassness, expediency, and, whenever possible, deception. He was not above telling any female that he loved her. My mother was out of her league in this place. Sophisticated intrigues and deceptions practiced by mature people in French restaurants were about par for her stage of life. But she needed to be rescued from the minor-league advances of a sweating adolescent in a pizza parlor.

I wanted to go. I also wanted to stay. Travis's arm occasionally brushed against mine as we ate. It was accidental but nice. I liked the idea that he wasn't out with a girl, but I wondered why he was friendly with Duane. Duane deserved to be a social outcast, but he wasn't.

My mother suddenly decided that the evening was over. We had almost finished our pizzas anyway. Having transported Amy and Linda to this place, she made sure that they had rides home. She made sure that she paid for the pizzas. She was a responsible adult. But we made a rather jerky, abrupt departure. She had stood up and said, "Time to go." You'd think she was Cinderella afraid to overstay her alloted time.

Travis said good night to me in a friendly way. Everyone said thanks to my mother. Outside, my mother said, "I felt right at home with your friends."

"You did?"

"Yes. That poor Duane fellow has an annoying knee tremor. It's probably a minor neurological disorder, but his parents should take care of it."

"Is that why you left abruptly?"

"It wasn't abrupt. I met your friends and now they're aware that you come from a family rooted in the community. The word will get around that you do have a mother."

"Did you do this so that my friends could see my roots?"

"Jody, you have a mother who cares about you. Let's not keep it under wraps."

I sighed. I didn't want to keep my mother under wraps. But I didn't want to advertise her in neon lights either. A little moderation, please.

She drove us home. Mom, benefactress, pal, fan of all-American humanoids, she thought the evening was an unqualified success. She had done wondrous things for her daughter, hadn't she? Motherhood administered by a sledgehammer. She had done awkwardly something she wanted to do well. But in an odd sort of way, the evening had worked. Not because it turned out well, but because it didn't. I was touched by how much she wanted to be my mother again, and I felt closer to her.

6

Matt's idea for a super Sunday was to go for a scenic drive and take some pictures under the bright autumn leaves.

I watched for his car Sunday morning. When it pulled up, I ran outside. I didn't wait for him to come into my house. I didn't want him to have to face my mother. He smiled when he saw me come out of the house and run toward him. He was wearing a nubby brown sweater that gave him a new-season look, and I thought how lucky I was to share this brisk fall day with someone like him. There are some days when you especially feel you're in love. The first day of spring, I guess, but that's so conventional. Valentine's Day? Well, it's expected of you. I'd cast my vote for a fall day when you see someone in a brown sweater waiting for you in a car.

As we drove off, I said, "We now have a two-season

relationship. Summer and autumn. I met you on the first day of my summer vacation from school, and now summer's gone and everything's leafy and we're still together. Do you think we'll ever share a winter snowflake?"

Matt grinned. "Have you been watching soap operas? My mother watches them and then she starts to talk like you. Sometimes I sit and watch. I get hooked. All those characters drinking coffee and chatting into eternity while they discover and rediscover The First Whiff of Spring in the Air, The First Falling Leaves, The Imminent First Snowflake, and Infidelity. All the basics."

"Oh, Matt, it's dumb, but it's romantic, too."

"Romantic? My mother filled me in on some of the plots. One main character has been married on television four times. Two divorces, one drowning, and one jump from the window of an asylum had disposed of his former wives. He's getting married again. *Five* wives, refills always available. His sister, another main character, wise and unerring, warned him against wives number two and four, but he wouldn't listen."

"Please. Let's not talk about wives and marital problems. It's too close to home. My home, anyway."

"Mine too. Whatever happens in your home is now going to affect mine. Okay, agreed. Let's just appreciate this remarkable day."

Matt drove into the country. The scenery was gorgeous. We found a beautiful spot for taking pictures. He stopped the car and we got out. He slung his camera strap over his shoulder and we walked toward a huge old tree. Matt was looking around.

"What are you looking for?"

"Someone to take our picture together."

"We passed some people a few trees back."

"Yes, but the scenery wasn't as good. Oh, well. Go smile under that old tree."

I smiled under the old tree. Matt snapped my picture.

"Nice! Hold it. I'll take some more."

"Same pose?"

"Turn slightly to the right. Look happy."

"Like this?"

"Like that."

Matt kept snapping. He would have used his whole roll up on me. But I stopped him. "Let me take you now. Smiling under the tree, of course."

"Of course."

Matt smiled under the tree. I took a few pictures.

"Stop!" he said. "That's enough of me."

"We have five shots left," I said. "Let's save them. It's getting too cold out here to pose."

"I'll keep you warm," said Matt, and he put his arm around me as we walked back to the car.

We drove on until we found a restaurant. We ordered, of all things, chicken soup.

"Why are we eating this?" I asked.

"Beats me."

It was a silly perfect morning. Until we drove back to my house and I invited him inside. I felt invigorated and happy, and I figured that he had to meet

my mother sometime. Why not on this wonderful
day?

We walked into the house. My father wasn't in
sight. My mother was measuring kitchen cabinets
with a tape measure. Was she planning a new
kitchen?

"Mom, I'd like you to meet Matt Green."

Matt and I were standing in the doorway to the
kitchen.

My mother put her tape measure down and
smiled. "I'm so happy to meet you," she said.

"It's nice to meet you, too," Matt answered.

There didn't seem to be anything else they wanted
to say to each other. I supplied, "Matt and I have
been taking pictures."

"Pictures?" said my mother. "Don't mention pictures. I'm so behind with them. Is that a new camera?
When you get a new camera, you snap and snap, but
eventually the novelty wears thin and the camera
gathers dust. Years and years go by and chances are
gone. I took all sorts of pictures of Jody when she was
growing up, but then I got lazy."

My mother also skipped the country.

She went on, "Any shots left in your camera? I'd
love to have some family pictures."

"There are five left," Matt said.

"Would you mind terribly?" my mother asked.
"Gerald's upstairs. I'll get him. And if it's not a tre-
mendous imposition, could you take Gerald and Jody
and me together? A family picture."

Matt did mind, terribly. I could see that he did. But my mother left the room to get my father.

"I'm supposed to *record* this family reunion?" he said. "*Me* take pictures of the loving Mr. and Mrs. Kline and their daughter? No thanks."

Matt walked toward the front door.

"Please, Matt."

He put his hand on the doorknob. "Understand," he said, "I'm not angry at *you*. But my mother is planning to marry your father and now, apparently, he's taken your mother back."

"Not really. She's just in the house in her role as my mother. That's all. Besides, didn't you want your mother to remarry your father? Isn't this a chance for them to get together again?"

"There's nothing I'd want more than a remarriage between my folks. Unfortunately that possibility has cooled off and died thanks to your father. But if your mother doesn't move out of the house, I guarantee that my mother and your father are finished. My mother won't put up with it."

"I can't make my mother move out. And I think I want her to stay. I don't know yet. It's a tough time for me."

"Then your dad should move out."

"Now, wait a minute. You want either my mother or my father to move out of this house?"

"That's it."

"Who are you to give commands?"

"I'm not giving commands."

"Yes, you are!"

Matt opened the door and strode to his car. The crazy thing about it was that I wasn't really angry at him. I was frustrated by the whole situation. Matt was probably right. It seemed to me that *somebody* should move out of the house. But I didn't know who.

As I closed the front door, I changed my mind about Matt. I was mad at him. I was mad at everybody. Matt, my parents, Gossamer, Uncle Mike, the whole works. It was irrational, but it felt good to be irrational.

I went upstairs and told my parents that their photographer had gone home.

7

I went to my room, wrote down all my feelings, and mailed them to Mrs. Opal O'Malley Spiegel Stamp of Montana. Opal was my friend. I had met her the same day I met Matt and his mother. She was a middle-aged lady who had rung my doorbell to do market research on deodorants. I reluctantly let her in. She was pushy, but kind. Eventually, during the summer, I confided in her. She confided in me. She was a part-time poet and she let me read her most personal thoughts, which she called "Fragments." She was like a substitute mother. But then she'd got married and moved to Montana. I missed her. I really missed her. We exchanged letters. But it wasn't the same as talking to her in person.

I read over my letter to Opal.

Dear Opal,

My mother came home. She spent two years traveling around the world to find herself. I just found myself. An angry person, that's what I found. I'm mad at the following people: my mother, my father, Matt Green, Gossamer Green, and Uncle Mike. You've never heard of Uncle Mike unless they have one of his fitness franchises in Montana. Come back to New York, Opal.

Love,
Jody

Writing the letter made me feel better. I put it in an envelope, addressed the envelope, sealed it, stamped it, and took it to a mailbox. I took my sketchpad and pencil with me. After I mailed the letter, I went to the park. I didn't want to spend the afternoon in my house.

I walked up to an elderly man who was sitting on a bench. "Excuse me," I said, "but I'm an artist and I'd like to draw your picture."

The man was flattered. He turned his face in various directions. "Which way?" he asked.

"Whatever feels comfortable."

I sat down beside him and started to sketch. "How's it going?" he asked every few minutes.

"Fine," I kept saying.

"The chin is wrong."

A voice intruded on us. Travis was standing over me! "The chin is wrong," he repeated. "This gentleman's chin projects. In your picture, it recedes. Here, want me to fix it?"

"No!"

The man chuckled. "You two fighting over my chin? No one ever fought over my chin before. Come to the park. Get a new experience."

Travis sat down beside me. He kept staring at the picture. But he kept quiet.

"It must be killing you to keep your thoughts to yourself," I said. "Say something, Picasso."

"It's quite good. Except for the chin."

I studied the picture. He was right about the chin. I could take criticism. I changed the chin. "How's that?" I asked.

"Don't ask him, ask me. It's my chin," said the man.

"Sorry," I said. I handed the picture to the man.

"Perfect," he said.

I smiled. "It's yours."

"Thank you, miss. And thank you, young man, for the chin."

I turned to Travis. "You were indispensable," I said sarcastically.

"Don't mention it."

"I'd rather not." I got up and walked away.

Travis came after me. "I was only trying to help. Look how pleased that man is with his picture."

"So? Do you think you're some kind of expert?"

"Well, I make money with my portraits, if that means anything."

"Money? How? Do you have a gallery that shows them?"

"No, nothing that magnificent. I do dogs."

"Dogs?"

"Yeah, dog portraits. It's a potentially big market. Some people will pay more money for a portrait of their dog than for a portrait of a husband or wife. It's incredible."

"Are you putting me on?"

"Serious. A friend once asked me to draw his dog's picture. Just as a favor. So I did. Then he showed it to a lady who said she'd like to have *her* dog done. So I did her dog for twenty-five bucks. Then I put up ads around town for dog portraits at, get this, one hundred dollars per, and I've been doing steady business. I also do oil paintings. For those I charge two fifty. But the black-and-white sketches for one hundred are where the action's at. I'm telling you that people are nuts about their dogs, and they put their money where their devotion is."

"How do you have time to do all the pictures and be vice-president of the senior class?"

Travis gave me a suspicious look. "You know me? Are you a senior?"

"Junior."

I stared back at him. He was wearing his bulky jacket and he looked very rugged. He had a fierce strong face. It was hard for that face to look friendly. But he seemed to be trying.

"I'm going to meet a dog owner to discuss a sitting," he said. "Want to come?"

"How does a dog sit?"

He laughed. I was getting to like him. I didn't want him to leave. Oh, Matt, what was going on? I wasn't sure that I was in love with Matt anymore. Right there, standing in the park, I wasn't sure anymore.

We were a few feet from the bench where the man was still admiring his picture. The man called to us, "Hey, you two young artists, you make a handsome pair."

"I agree," Travis yelled back.

He was too sure of himself. I liked that about him and I didn't. But I hoped he wouldn't walk away without me.

"Coming?" He turned to me.

"Where does this dog live?"

"A few streets away. He has a nice house." Travis laughed again. "One thing, though. The dog's name is Poopsie. Please get used to that right now so you won't laugh when you hear it. The dog is owned by this lady Mrs. Ronstone who adores him. The way she said Poopsie over the phone when she called to make the appointment . . . P—oooo-psie, like that . . . well, get used to it. I don't want to offend her."

We walked along. I wondered why he didn't say anything about last night at the pizzeria. Was he so busy criticizing my portrait and talking about Mrs. Ronstone's dog that he forgot? I wanted last night to be forgettable, but more likely it was indelible.

Mrs. Ronstone's household was a pocket of insanity in an otherwise sane neighborhood. I'm not saying this with any disrespect, because we all need something by which to measure our own sanity. Mrs. Ronstone allowed her dog to run her household. I knew that, before Travis and I even got inside. I recognized her house from last summer when Alison and I were collecting cans for charity. Poopsie had tried to bite Alison, and Mrs. Ronstone had given us a dozen cans, out of guilt or out of generosity. A rolled newspaper smack on Poopsie's bottom would have been a better gesture.

Mrs. Ronstone answered her door right away. Except for letting Poopsie rule her life, she seemed like an intelligent woman. As she greeted us at the door, she looked stern and businesslike, the way librarians and schoolteachers used to be depicted on TV before the real librarians and schoolteachers complained. Poopsie was there beside her. He didn't seem to be in a biting mood. He was a beautiful long-haired white sheepdog type, the kind that always gets parts in family movies. The idea was that if you hate a dog like this, you hate all of humanity.

Travis introduced me as "Jody, who's also an artist." I guess he felt funny about just bringing a girl along. Mrs. Ronstone didn't remember me from the can collecting.

Back to insanity. Mrs. Ronstone wanted to discuss "appropriate backgrounds" for Poopsie's portrait. Why not? This was a portrait of royalty, or at least "head of household."

We walked around the house looking for the perfect place.

"Is morning light or afternoon light better?" Mrs.

Ronstone asked. "And before or after meals? Sometimes Poopsie appears a bit sluggish after he eats."

Travis and Mrs. Ronstone decided to pose Poopsie on his favorite blanket. How they would get this nervous dog to stay there and pose was not discussed. Mrs. Ronstone then tried to lower the price to ninety dollars. Travis, surprisingly, agreed. He hadn't mentioned that dog lovers might stoop to price haggling. It was settled. My parents' marriage was up in the air, my relationship with Matt was shaky, Gossamer Green and Big Mike loomed as question marks in my parents' lives, and I was never sure anymore who would be living in my house by the time I got home. Yet it was settled that Poopsie was going to pose on his beloved blanket for the fee of ninety dollars, bringing incalculable pleasure to the household of Mrs. Ronstone. There *are* answers to some problems.

Mrs. Ronstone started to ask Travis about frames for the portrait he had yet to draw. I hung back while they talked. I looked around. The house was shabby. I was sure it had once been nice. It was full of old things. I wondered if Mrs. Ronstone could afford the ninety dollars for the picture.

I wandered into the kitchen. My mother would have remodeled that kitchen without thinking twice. Off the kitchen was a little den or something. A man was sitting there reading a newspaper. He was wearing a dark green flannel bathrobe. His back was toward me. He was probably Mrs. Ronstone's husband or boyfriend. None of my business. But then I happened to look just below the hem of his bathrobe,

Ordinarily one would expect to see bedroom slippers or bare feet or something bathrobe-appropriate. But this man was wearing crew socks and blazing white sneakers. He was Uncle Mike!

8

It couldn't be Uncle Mike. Where did he say he lived? In a penthouse in a skyscraper in New York City. And his business offices were in the city, too. He had given the impression that he had come in from the city to see my mother. What was he doing in his bathrobe a few streets away? Maybe it wasn't Uncle Mike. Bathrobes, crew socks, and sneakers could be a new fashion. I'm not up on these things. The man's back was still toward me. I started to walk into the den for a closer look.

"Young lady," said Mrs. Ronstone, suddenly appearing in the kitchen. "Please don't disturb my boarder."

I felt like a sneak who had been caught.

Travis was ready to leave. He was patting Poopsie. "See you next week, fella." Then he said to me, "I'm coming back next Sunday to start the picture."

"Poopsie and I are looking forward to it," said Mrs. Ronstone as she showed us to the door.

Outside, I asked, "Have you been here before?"

"No, I only talked to her on the phone."

"So you don't know who her boarder is?"

"Should I? I didn't know she had one. She's a widow who probably needs some extra bread. Anything unusual about that?"

"No, of course not. Well, I guess I'll be going home now."

"I'll walk you."

We started to walk. "That was fun," I said. "Thanks for asking me."

"I'd like to ask you someplace else. Want to go out sometime?"

"You mean a date?"

"Yeah, with no dogs."

"Uh . . ."

"You don't want to?"

"This is going to sound strange. I've been going steady, but I may not be as of a few hours ago."

"You're right. It does sound strange."

"There's a guy I've been dating, but it's a mixed-up situation and . . ."

"Is that why you were out with your mother last night?"

There it was. He hadn't forgotten. Who could forget my mother's behavior?

"My mother and I went to the movies. She enjoys mingling with my friends. But getting back to us, I mean, your asking me out, could I think it over? I don't want to put you off, but I can't say yes right now."

"Okay, don't try to explain. I get it."

He was trying to be agreeable, but there was something conceited about him. Arrogant. Maybe it was just his manner.

When we got home to my house, he did something that shocked me. He leaned over and kissed me! I hardly knew him and the sun was shining and we were right in front of my house and I associate kisses with knowing somebody and a little darkness and subtlety. But I *liked* the kiss. If I had ever been in love with Matt, I was afraid I wasn't anymore. That wasn't saying anything against Matt. It was saying something against myself. I couldn't trust my feelings. Maybe I was as mixed up as my mother and father with their indecision and lack of commitment. Maybe I inherited it.

Travis said, "I like you," and he turned and left.

I went into the house. I heard my mother and father in the kitchen. I started up toward my room. I changed my mind. I went into the living room. I walked over to the sofa where Uncle Mike had sat a few days ago. I peered down at the section where he had been sitting. I rubbed my fingers over it. Nothing. I got some transparent tape from a desk in the den. I pressed the sticky side of the tape to the sofa. Some things stuck to the tape. Long white dog hairs. Poopsie's hairs! They had to be. We didn't have a dog. Betty, our maid, didn't have a dog. Some of my friends have dogs, but I don't entertain my friends on the living room sofa. It's mainly for grown-ups. I wasn't Sherlock Holmes, but I was still able to make deductions. People who live in houses with dogs can become carriers of dog hair. They pick up, they deposit, without even being aware of it. Poopsie the sheepdog was a formidable shedder. These dog hairs confirmed what I already knew. Uncle Mike lived with, or was staying with, Mrs. Ronstone. Did my mother know? Someone was being deceitful. There was a plot of sorts, but whose and why, I didn't know.

I went upstairs and thought about my recent kiss.

9

Matt phoned that night.

"Are you angry at me?" That was the first thing he asked.

"Well, I wasn't, then I was, but now I'm not."

"Good." Matt hesitated. Then he said, "Look, I'm going to take my mother out next weekend."

"Next weekend? But you're supposed to see *me* next weekend. Do you mean the entire weekend?"

I didn't want to hear his answer. Somehow I didn't want to hear his answer.

"Jody, this is so hard to say, but okay, here it is. I think we should let our parents work out their problems."

I felt relieved. "So do I," I said. "I agree. So what's this about the weekend?"

Matt hesitated again. "Jody, try to understand. It's just too painful for me to see you right now. I think we should stand back and *wait* until everything has fallen into place."

"I don't understand."

"It's my mother. She's very upset about your mother's return. She seems to think of you and your mother as one person. The enemy camp. And I'm caught in the middle. It won't be forever. I guess what I'm asking from you is patience."

"Patience?" Matt didn't understand how *I* felt. He only knew how his mother felt.

He went on talking. "Just a little patience until this matter is resolved."

"Resolved? That's lawyer talk."

"Jody, I'm trying—"

"Know something? I'm not crazy about my father being a lawyer and now I'm not crazy about your wanting to be one. It's more than a profession. It's a frame of mind."

"Look, I guess this has hit you out of the blue. Try to relax. I care about you. I shouldn't have to say that anymore. You should know by now. I'll call you in a week or so and see how you're feeling."

"Now you sound like a doctor. You forgot the part about taking two aspirin."

I was being sarcastic, I knew it. But it kept me from crying, right there over the phone. I wanted Matt to see how badly I was hurt, and yet I didn't want him to see. Everything was falling apart. His mother was in a rotten situation. I couldn't deny that. But what about me? I needed him, too.

He said, "Jody, please . . ." Was he pleading? I hoped so.

I said, "Good-bye, Matt."

I hung up and cried. I forgot all about my afternoon kiss. My head was full of Matt. I remembered the first time I met him, when he came to my house for dinner. After that, there had been ups and downs. I thought the downs were over with.

It was all my parents' fault. I wanted to have a talk with my father, the kind we used to have before my mother came home. But there was never a chance anymore. He had given up on our weekly father-daughter dinners at restaurants, too. Either my mother was around or she seemed to be around. She was part of the new atmosphere. I couldn't tell if they were getting closer. Around me, they were on guard. Gossamer, of course, had stopped coming to the house. I could only guess that my father was taking her out in the city.

Dinnertime. We were having a Sunday-night family dinner, the three of us. My mother had made most of it. Steak, salad, and some éclairs from the bakery.

We were eating our éclairs when the doorbell rang. "I'll get it," I said. It could be Matt, sorry about the phone call and trying to make up in person. It could be Travis, wanting another kiss.

I opened the door. Uncle Mike was standing there. My eyes shot down to his feet. If he was wearing ordinary shoes and stockings, then maybe he wasn't the crew-socks-and-sneakers guy I saw this afternoon at Mrs. Ronstone's house. Uncle Mike was not wear-

ing ordinary shoes and stockings. Once again, the
crew socks and blazing white sneakers.

"I'm a bit early," he said. "It's hard to figure your
way through traffic."

What traffic? I wondered. Didn't he come from a
few streets away?

My mother heard him. She rushed to greet him.
"Uncle Mike," she said, and she gave him a little
peck-kiss on the cheek. My father, curious about our
absence, joined us. My mother introduced Uncle
Mike to my father as follows: "Gerald, meet Uncle
Mike. Would you believe we met in London? He's
not my uncle, of course. You may have heard of the
Uncle Mike Fitness Camps. Well, this is the founder
and president."

My mother was proud of Uncle Mike and his string
of fitness-camp accomplishments.

Uncle Mike extended his hand toward my father.
My father didn't take it. How could my father be so
rude to this stranger! My father must be jealous. That
was the only reason I could think of. Maybe my
mother was trying to *make* him jealous. Think about
it, Jody. Uncle Mike had been sitting on the sofa
when I got home from school the day after my
mother returned. Then he left almost immediately.
He was there just long enough for me to meet him.
No, that's not fair. It might have been coincidental
that he left right after I met him. My mother had
disclaimed that she had any romantic interest in him.
Could she have arranged for me to know of Uncle
Mike's existence, then played it cool, hoping I'd tell

my father about Uncle Mike, which I didn't do? Now he showed up on a Sunday night, near the end of a planned family dinner when my mother knew my father would be here.

Then there was the matter of Mrs. Ronstone's boarder. It made no sense at all for him to be Uncle Mike. And yet the sneakers, the crew socks, the dog hair, all pointed to it.

Suddenly I was scared. I was scared for my father. My mother and Uncle Mike had probably cooked up a scheme to make my father jealous. It wasn't like my mother. She was flighty, but she wasn't devious. Still, she'd been gone two years. People change.

My mother and Uncle Mike left. He had come by to pick her up and take her out. I immediately said to my father, "Mom said he's just a friend. This isn't a date or anything. It's just two friends."

My father looked disturbed. "When did she tell you that? Has this Uncle Mike been here before?"

"Yes, the day after Mom got back. When I got home from school, he was sitting on our sofa. You're jealous, aren't you? You still love Mom. It's okay if you still love Mom."

"I'm not jealous," he said. I noticed that he didn't comment on the other part of my observation. Then he added, "Believe me, I'm not jealous of Uncle Mike."

At the time, I didn't believe him. I thought he was and he didn't know it.

We went back to our éclairs. My mother hadn't finished hers. "Dad," I said, "I think Mom is trying to get you back. She's trying to make you jealous with this Uncle Mike. So, are you ready to choose between Mom and Gossamer?"

"Gossamer still wants to marry me." My father said it with some pride. And then I knew. My father had two women after him, and he loved the idea. How could he? He was a grown man. But he was a hurt grown man. My mother had walked out on him. Now obviously she wanted him back or she wouldn't have moved into the house. And Gossamer wanted him, too. My father was reveling in the simple human joy of being wanted.

He changed the subject. "What about you, Jody? How are things with Matt?"

I shook my head negatively. I couldn't answer.

"Problems, huh? It's my fault. He probably thinks I'm being unfair to his mother, and it's affecting his relationship with you."

"You *are* being unfair to his mother, Dad. I've never been wild about Gossamer, but I've accepted her. You can't leave her dangling like this."

"Jody . . ." My father hesitated. Then he said, "Down deep, do you want your mother and me back together?"

I shrugged. "When Mom walked out on us, she picked what made her happy. Now you pick what makes you happy. It's your turn, Dad."

"Then you don't want me to make a decision based on you?"

"No!"

My father stood up, walked to my side of the table,

bent down, and hugged me. Then he said, "If Uncle Mike comes to the house while I'm out, don't open the door for him. I don't want that man inside my home again, and I'm telling your mother that."

My father was reclaiming his house. It was a good first step. And yet, what did he have against this stranger, this Uncle Mike?

10

My mother cornered me the next morning before I left for school. Maybe *cornered* isn't the right word, but she was up very early waiting for me. My father had just left for work. I had a feeling that the two of them had already had a long conversation that morning. I couldn't tell by her expression whether it had turned out well or not.

"Got a few minutes?" she asked.

"Sure."

I was eager to hear what she would say. Maybe she would tell me all about Uncle Mike.

We faced each other across the breakfast table.

"What do you think of me?" she asked. Just like that.

I hesitated. It wasn't a simple question.

Maybe she didn't expect an answer. She went right on. "I put that badly. Anyway, I think I know the answer. I'm someone who took off without notice, traveled all over the world, and came home. You think I'm treating the whole thing as if I went out to the supermarket on a whim to buy a cake, stayed a little longer than expected, and then returned."

"Sometimes it does seem that way, Mom."

"Okay, Jody. I know what I did was very, very *serious.* I left. I hurt you and your father. But I didn't do it frivolously. It wasn't a lark."

"You could have warned us."

"No. Your father would have tried to talk me out of it. He *would* have talked me out of it. But then, a few months later, he would have had to do it all over again."

"So you just took off."

"Just took off? Oh, no. It was a long, slow process. Reaching the point of actually leaving, well, it didn't happen overnight, Jody. When you get to be an adult, when you get to be my age, you can begin to feel very stale. You start wondering if you're missing something. And you keep *on* wondering. This is the way I was."

"I'm confused. You felt *stale?* I thought you left home to find yourself."

My mother sighed. She seemed frustrated. She was trying so hard to tell me something, and it wasn't going the way she wanted it to go.

But she kept trying. "It's all tied together. Understand that I'm not complaining about the life I had here. It wasn't without love, certainly. It wasn't without its satisfactions, and one of the best parts, one of the very best parts, was watching you grow. But I wanted to see *me* grow."

"You grow by leaving home? I don't buy that. Anyhow, *grow* has become a cop-out word to excuse the way a person acts."

"I did grow. Don't I seem different to you now? Don't you think I've changed?"

"Not really. The only way you seem different is that I know living inside you is a person who was capable of leaving home for two years. Honestly, Mom, I'm not being sarcastic. I wish I could explain it better. I'll try. Let's take Fred Astaire."

"Fred Astaire?"

"Yeah. I saw him in an old movie on TV the other night. He had this fabulous ability to dance, this fantastic talent living inside him just waiting to break out. Well, it's like you had this big, fantastic thing living inside you, this urge to leave, and I was your daughter and didn't even know about it. Well, now I know about it, and that's what's changed, my knowing about it."

My mother smiled faintly. "Fair enough," she said.

I pushed my chair back. It was time to leave for school. "Have you told Dad what you told me?"

"Sure. I also told him that I'm very contented being back. But it's a slow process, trying to mend something. Your father and I know that."

I wanted to ask her what kind of mending was going on. I wanted to ask her about Uncle Mike, too. Another day.

11

At school I expected Travis to "find" me. I thought he would see me and come over. I didn't see him, but that didn't mean that he didn't catch sight of me. Anyway, no luck.

Tuesday was the same. I don't know why I was waiting to be found. Actually, I was supposed to let Travis know whether I'd go out with him. I had decided that I'd accept. Matt decided for me, I guess.

On Wednesday I was actively looking for Travis. There is a lot to be said for this hard-to-get business. He may not have been playing hard to get, but the result was the same. The more I didn't see him, the more I wanted to see him. I definitely wanted to go out on a date with him. I also hoped he'd invite me to go to Mrs. Ronstone's house with him on Sunday. I had to find out about her boarder.

I was getting more and more concerned about Uncle Mike. I knew something about him that my mother did or didn't know. Mrs. Ronstone's boarder was passing himself off as tycoon Uncle Mike. If my mother knew, then she and this man had cooked up a scheme to make my father jealous. It was bizarre, it was deceitful, and it would probably be the end of any chance my mother had of getting my father back. My father deserved better. I would have to tell him what I knew. But I wasn't ready. I didn't know enough.

I wrote another letter to Opal. I told her about Uncle Mike, and I asked her opinion about how my mother, after only one day back in town, would know Mrs. Ronstone's boarder. My mother wasn't even acquainted with Mrs. Ronstone, as far as I knew. But Opal, as a door-to-door ringer of doorbells and professional observer of people, might have some insight into how seemingly unconnected people might have connected. Opal had an overview of life.

On Thursday I found myself running down a hall at school, calling Travis's name. I had caught sight of him, finally.

He turned. He stopped. He smiled when he recognized me. I wondered if he remembered that he asked me for a date. When I caught up with him, I blurted out, "I'd like to go out with you."

"Your timing is great. All the junior and senior class officers are invited to a party a week from Saturday night. Want to go with me?"

I hated the way he said, "all the junior and senior class officers." It sounded so important. Maybe there

wasn't another way of saying it. What was he supposed to say: "Aw shucks, gee whiz, heck, it seems
that the junior and senior officers have been, oh,
golly, invited to a party"?

"I'm not a class officer," I said.

"Doesn't matter. We can invite guests. It's just a
party given by somebody who's got a thing for class
officers, I guess."

"I'd love to go," I said. "Who's giving the party?"

In the next second or two I would learn that I had
answered Travis in the wrong order. My answer
should have been: "Who's giving the party?" *Then*, if
the answer was satisfactory, I would say, "I'd love to
go."

"Tanya Lipsert," said Travis.

12

I felt myself getting closer to my mother. She was easing back into her old role as Mom. I was getting used to her again. Bit by bit she told me about her travels. I even enjoyed some of the stories, stories about places that had separated her from me.

Betty went about the house doing her chores, loyally pretending that my mother had never been away. Were my father and I in the process of wiping out those two years, too?

I told Alison about Uncle Mike. I couldn't wait for an answer from Opal. I had a sense of urgency.

Alison lives a boring life, going steady with Pete Summers year after year, so she welcomed the idea of a conspiracy between my mother and Uncle Mike. I would have been angry about Alison's insensitivity, but really, she needed something spicy and malicious in her dull existence. Pete Summers had bored an otherwise good person into becoming a desperate searcher for scandalous tidbits.

Alison was sitting on my bed. Her eyes were shining.

"This is hot stuff," she said.

"Control yourself, Alison. You'll burn up."

"Not before I find out what happens."

"I don't know how to find out *anything*."

"Just wondering about it will get you nowhere."

"True."

Alison's eyes were still shining. "Every day we can walk by Mrs. Ronstone's house on the way to school."

"It's not on the way to school."

"We can make it on the way. A daily routine. If we do that, maybe we'll catch sight of Uncle Mike coming or going."

"And maybe we won't. We could walk by for months and not see anything."

"Possible. How about Travis? Would he let you go along for the portrait session on Sunday?"

"I thought of that. But he didn't ask. Mrs. Ronstone didn't seem overjoyed when I showed up last time. Especially when I started to wander into her den."

"Couldn't you offer to go as his helper? Hold his sketching pencils or something?"

"Oh, sure. Next."

"Maybe we could collect cans again and see if we can get inside. Forget it. Her dog doesn't like me."

"It's okay, Alison. I appreciate the thought. If you come up with anything, let me know."

"But I came up with gems. *Gems!*"

After Alison left, I straightened up my room and tried to forget Uncle Mike. There didn't seem to be anything I could do about him. Alison's ideas seemed so juvenile. I was beginning to feel like an over-imaginative schoolgirl, jumping to farfetched conclusions.

I don't know how I got the idea that I got next. It was simple, it was to the point. I left the house. I walked to Mrs. Ronstone's house. I knew what I was looking for. Uncle Mike's car. The gray-blue sports car I had seen parked in front of my house the day I met him. I hadn't given it a thought the day I was at Mrs. Ronstone's with Travis.

Now as I approached Mrs. Ronstone's house, I saw that there was no car parked in front of it. I walked to the driveway. The gray-blue sports car was parked there, sitting like a revelation under the matching gray-blue of the afternoon sky.

13

Postponing unpleasant jobs is, I suppose, a form of cowardice. I of course had to tell my father about the Uncle Mike deception. But by telling myself that I needed the right time, place, and atmosphere, I put it off. Then I thought about telling my mother that I knew her business executive friend from New York City was actually a boarder at Mrs. Ronstone's house a few streets away. My mother would have the chance to do the honorable thing and clear out, giving my father and Gossamer a clear future. But I didn't do that, either.

I wrapped myself up in my own life. I went to Tanya Lipsert's party with Travis. This was the first date I'd had with anyone other than Matt since I met him. I refused to acknowledge a blind date Alison had once arranged on a disastrous summer night as a real date.

Travis arrived at my door wearing a yellow shirt and khakis, looking as casual as a member of the establishment could. Where was the artist I had met in the park?

If only we weren't going to Tanya's house. That was the downer. "Does Tanya know you invited me?" I asked when we were in his car.

"No. She said we could bring guests. You're my guest."

"Will it be a big party?"

"Depends upon how many guests the main guests invite."

"Main guests?"

"The class officers."

"Oh, that's right."

"Are you in the spirit of this, or are you somewhere else?"

"In the spirit."

"Great."

At Tanya's house I walked hesitantly up the front steps with Travis. But as he rang the doorbell, I had the happy thought that Tanya would be unpleasantly shocked to see me with Travis. He was considered such a catch at school. Maybe she was even trying to catch him herself. My spirits lifted considerably as the door opened, and fell considerably when I saw Matt Green standing there.

14

I introduced Matt and Travis. Now I had a chance to compare them up close. I thought about the pastry carts that are wheeled around in fancy restaurants so that diners can choose a dessert from them. The desserts are always so gorgeous and mouth-watering that instead of choosing, you just gape and admire. Matt and Travis were clearly of pastry-cart caliber.

Tanya appeared, smiled, and took Matt's arm. He was her selection. For her, there was nothing else on the cart.

Matt was so surprised to see me that instead of saying hello, he asked, "What are you doing here?" He knew that I wouldn't voluntarily attend a party of Tanya's. Apparently, he would. He wasn't hand-cuffed, chained, or visibly beaten. He had come be-cause he wanted to. Or because he had nothing else to do on a Saturday night. Or because Mr. Lipsert had suggested it at the office. I consoled myself by thinking that he had simply accepted an invitation. He hadn't asked Tanya out. Had he?

I answered his question. "Travis invited me."

Matt was sizing up Travis. "Travis is an artist," I added. I wanted to hurt Matt by showing that Travis and I had something important in common. But the remark was so out of place that I could have just as logically announced that Travis had an ingrown toenail.

Travis laughed. He was embarrassed.

"He makes money at it," I added. Something inside me, the something that had charge of the movement of my tongue, was my enemy.

Travis laughed again. He probably wanted to take me home. We had been at the party for less than a minute. We were still standing in the doorway.

Travis explained to Matt. "I do dog portraits. There's good money in dogs."

"Dogs, huh?" Matt seemed interested.

"The portraits probably won't win any prizes, but I don't care. Most prizes in the arts are awarded when the recipient is too old to stand up and accept them, anyway. If you literally are so feeble you can't walk unassisted up to a stage to accept an award, everyone thinks you deserve to get it. The award is for living so long."

Matt stroked his chin. "Yeah, the most applause does go to the people who have to be helped up to the stage. You're right."

"I am."

I was standing there, not saying a word. I was completely out of the conversation that I had started.

Tanya tugged at Matt's arm. "Let's go back down to the party."

Tanya led the way downstairs to her basement. Matt, Travis, and I followed. "Food's over there," Tanya said, pointing to a table at one end of the room.

"Want something?" Travis asked me.

"Something tall and cool," I said. "Cola, maybe."

"Be right back."

Travis went to get soda. I stood to the side and watched the room fill up slowly. Most of the guests were from school. Matt may have been the only one who wasn't. He and Tanya walked over to a couch. The room had several couches and various types of old furniture that looked too good for a garage sale but not good enough for upstairs. The doorbell rang and Tanya went back upstairs to greet more guests. Matt sat down on the couch alone.

"Cola coming up." Travis returned with two drinks. Then, nodding to me to come with him, he sat down near Matt on the couch. There was an empty space between them. I took it. Travis started to talk to Matt again over my head. They liked each other. It would have been more flattering to me if they hated each other. Please, guys, a *little* hatred.

Matt was now telling Travis how hectic it was to attend Columbia University and work part time in a law firm. Travis took in every word. I was waiting for them to exchange addresses and telephone numbers.

The other guests were doing sensible things like dancing. Tanya had a great stereo system. Duane Rabinowitz came over and asked me to dance. *Duane Rabinowitz?* He was a guest at this party? Say it isn't so.

I knew I looked available. I was sitting on a couch between two guys who were ignoring me.

"I'm not ready to dance, Duane," I said.

"What's to get ready? You look ready to me. You look needy."

Duane had a loud voice. I didn't want to talk to him, I didn't want to dance with him, I didn't want to be in the same room with him. But maybe he'd be satisfied with one dance and leave me alone for the rest of the evening. His plans for the evening were to go after every girl in the room. That's how he operated.

The music on the stereo was unfortunately slow and just right for close dancing. Duane and I started to dance close. Slow and close. He had these moving hands, and even if they weren't moving in the wrong places, there was something threatening about their moving at all.

He whispered in my ear, "I saved you from being ignored. I won't ignore you."

"I believe it."

"Want to go outside behind the house and talk about not being ignored?"

"I do not."

"Reconsider."

"No."

Duane was closing in on me. I had this totally rational fear that he was going to try to kiss me. His expression was emotional, expectant. He had the look of lust. He wore this look routinely in algebra class, in the cafeteria, in flag-raising ceremonies at the football stadium. In short, at all times. But now it was close to *me*. I was afraid that in a moment his mouth would be on mine. Yuck. It would be the clearest distortion of the function of a kiss since I was in the eighth grade and allowed myself to be embraced and kissed by zero Marty Frost at the end of a date, having been told by my girl friends that Marty's psyche would be mortally wounded if I shrank away.

Now I was pulling myself away from Duane with a minor amount of success. I looked toward the couch. Two possible rescuers weren't paying any attention to Duane and me. I was on my own. The dance was lasting forever.

Duane stepped on my foot. Was that an accident or not? I looked down at his feet. One of his socks had collapsed and I could see his anklebone revealed. I hoped it was the most intimate knowledge of his anatomy I would ever have.

I yanked myself out of his grasp. I wondered how he got himself invited to parties. I wondered how he managed to have any friends. It was a miracle. I went back to the couch.

Matt stopped talking to Travis. The second miracle. Matt actually stood up when he saw me, and he asked me to dance. Travis nodded as if to say it was okay.

I was out on the floor dancing with Matt. We were together again. But under the wrong circumstances. I said, "I accepted my invitation before I knew it was Tanya's party. What's your excuse?"

"She asked me at the office. Her father was standing there. It seemed like a friendly, harmless invitation. I'm not interested in her. Never was. Never will be."

"You don't have to explain to me."

"I want to. And I admit I want to know about Travis. Is he taking my place?"

"No, but every time I think about us, well, I wonder if there is an *us*. How come you don't want to see me but you're willing to see my father at the office?"

"That's business. In an office atmosphere I can be detached."

"So if I were business, you'd see me, too?"

"That's unfair."

"I guess it is."

"The last time I phoned you, you gave me the impression that you didn't even want me to call back. I'm unhappy about that."

"Who's unhappy? Not my special guest." Tanya was back. She put her hand on Matt's arm. He gave me an "I'm a helpless captive" look that was almost funny. Tanya led Matt away. She started to dance. Close to him. She was another Duane Rabinowitz. No wonder she'd invited Duane to her party. She had to take lessons from someone. She smiled up at Matt. Sweet. Manufactured sweet. What a put-on. We are gathered here tonight, ladies and gentlemen, to present the Academy Award to Tanya Lipsert for best performance of the evening and also for the entire body of her work.

Matt was Tanya's for the evening. I would live to fight another day.

Travis was still sitting on the couch. Two girls had sat down beside him. I went back to the couch and stood there. When the girls saw me, they excused themselves and left.

"Back?" said Travis.

"Back. You weren't lonely?"

"Not exactly."

"If you ask me to dance, I'll accept."

"Glad to hear that. I was beginning to think I'd have to stand in line."

Travis was a smooth dancer. A lot of the girls in the room were probably jealous of me. I was waiting for Travis to do or say something conceited, but he didn't. I hoped I had been wrong about him.

"Is Matt a good friend of yours?" he asked.

"What makes you think so?"

Had Matt said anything about me to Travis? It would be interesting to know.

"You two certainly act as if you're old friends or enemies or something. Is he your ex-boyfriend?"

Ex-boyfriend had a chilling sound to it. But maybe that's what Matt was.

"Maybe," I answered.

Travis seemed to dance a little closer after that.

15

Travis wanted to park in front of my house. I mean really park. He kissed me three times and he was just getting started.

"Travis . . ."

"Don't you like me?"

"Of course I like you."

"Well . . ."

"Well what?"

"Travis, we're in danger of having the quintessential parked-car conversation. That kind of conversation can ruin an evening."

"Great. So why talk?"

"You just kept up your end of it with a question like that." I sighed. "Look, here's the rundown. The minute a guy asks me if I like him, I figure he doesn't want to know. He just wants a cue for action."

Travis sat up straight. "Hey," he said, "who do you think I am? Duane Rabinowitz?"

"No, there's only one champ."

Travis got out of the car, came around and opened the door on my side. I got out. We walked up the stairs to my house.

"I'm not the kind of guy you think I am," he said. "You'll see."

He squeezed my arm and he left. I wondered if I'd see.

16

I had a plan for Sunday. I would do homework most of the day and then reward myself by starting a new painting. I like to reward myself for doing homework.

The doorbell rang at noon. My parents were out. My father had gone to his office to catch up on some work, and my mother was meeting a committee person for lunch. I opened the door.

A skinny girl with frizzy hair was standing there. She looked like she might be in her last year of selling Girl Scout cookies. She appeared to be eleven or twelve. I didn't recognize her.

"Hi," she said. "You Jody Kline?"

"Yes."

"Okay. I'm Dolly Bergstater, president of the Travis Cameo Fan Club. We've got the collective hots for Travis Cameo."

"You have what?"

"We have the collective hots for Travis Cameo."

I stood there, speechless. At last I asked, "Are you putting me on?"

"No. Can I come in?"

Dolly walked in while I was trying to decide whether or not she could come in. I invited her into the kitchen. The living room didn't seem to be the right place for her. She draped herself over a kitchen chair.

"Okay," she said, "we're a fan club of approximately twelve freshmen high school girls. We're sort of underground. That is, we don't advertise that we're a club, we don't advertise for members, but it gets around word of mouth. We rely heavily on word of mouth."

"I don't understand," I said. I draped myself over a chair too. "Dolly . . . that's your name? . . . what's the purpose of the club and why are you *here?*"

"Our purpose, as a group or one by one, is to get a date with the school hunk, Travis Cameo. None of us has succeeded so far, but *you* have. I was sent here to find out how you did it."

Dolly took out a notebook and pen. She was going to take notes!

"Back up," I said. "It's stupid to have a fan club for Travis Cameo. Why don't you girls get yourself a famous athlete or singer or something? Start a club for somebody famous or somebody on the way up. Not a guy from your own school."

"No. Think about it. Members of that kind of club

rarely, if ever, meet the star. They can't pick lint off his sweater, they can't see what he eats for dessert in the cafeteria, they can't share his true existence. But we in the Travis Cameo Fan Club, we're in a position to watch him every day. And did you know that one of us *touches* him every day on purpose? This Wednesday it's my turn again. I'll brush up against him outside of chemistry. I know the time and place."

"Does Travis know about the club?"

"Oh, no. He's conceited enough already." Dolly had her pen poised to write. "Do you think he's conceited?"

"I really—"

"Don't hesitate. You can tell me. He took you to Tanya Lipsert's party last night, didn't he? That's how we got your name."

"Who told you?"

"Please. We know these things. What kind of fan club would we be if we didn't know these things? Let's go back to the beginning. How did you meet Travis?"

"I don't have to tell you. I was just in the middle of doing my homework when you rang my bell. I don't want to be impolite but . . ."

"I'm sorry I interrupted your homework. But this is important not only to me, but to the rest of us. Come on, tell me how you met him. Do it for the sisterhood."

"What sisterhood?"

"Well, we're all girls . . ."

"Are you the most persuasive member of the club? Is that why they sent you?"

"We drew lots."

"Of course. Okay, I met Travis in the park. He was sketching a horse. I had a sketchbook with me. I was hoping to do a picture."

Dolly scribbled something in her notebook. "I knew it!" she said. "You met him when he was his brooding, artistic self. He sensed a common bond with you, a fellow artist."

"I'm not sure about that."

"It fits. It fits. He wouldn't have given you the time of day if he met you at school. So many girls go up to him at school and flirt but nothing happens. A sketchbook in the park. This information is priceless!"

"You're welcome to it. Do your parents know about this fixation? How much time do you give it?"

"We meet once a week. Most parents know about it because we each have a life-size blowup of Travis's picture on a wall. One of the members snapped him when he wasn't looking. But see, we don't do drugs, we don't drink, we don't smoke, and we have a clean and wholesome goal: a date with Travis Cameo."

"Yeah, well from a parent's point of view it could have a lot going for it. But frankly, I don't get it. Why are you doing this?"

"Simple. If you can't achieve something yourself, you attach yourself to somebody who can. Travis is an achiever."

"And you're not? I think you do quite well. You're here, you've learned how I met Travis . . ."

"Not enough. See, I'll never be a class officer, I'll never be a sex object. I'm too skinny, too blah, too nothing. But by connecting myself to Travis, I catch some of his fall-out."

"How did you get this low opinion of yourself, Dolly?"

"It's not all that low. It just seems that way because I have such a high opinion of Travis. It's the contrast."

"I thought you said he was conceited."

"Everyone's entitled to a flaw or two."

"You don't think he would have asked me out if he met me at school? Doesn't he date anyone he meets at school?"

"Not that we know of, and we should know. He thinks he's big stuff as an artist. Did he ever ask you along while he painted something? I bet he did."

"As a matter of fact there was this sheepdog—"

"You admire him as an artist, don't you?"

"He's very very good. That horse—"

"He wants to be admired that way. You fill a need. By the way, what park did you meet him in?"

"Sycamore Park. A few blocks from here."

Dolly wrote that down. "What day of the week, and the hour, please?"

"I can't remember. Wait, it was the day my mother . . . uh, it was a Tuesday, around three o'clock in the afternoon. There was still good light for drawing."

I offered Dolly a sandwich and a glass of milk. She accepted. "Dolly," I said as I made the sandwich, "what do you think of mass hysteria?"

"There's a lot to be said for it. Why?"

"Your club reminds me of it. You're thinking as a group. Now, truthfully, if you were all alone, would you take notes on Travis Cameo? Would you try to flick lint off his sweater?"

"Yes, absolutely."

"Oh."

Dolly munched on her sandwich. "I've got a question I'm not suppose to ask," she said. "But I have to know. How does he kiss?"

"How do you know he kissed me?"

"Guys that confident kiss girls."

Dolly was not without insight.

"He kisses okay. Really, that's personal."

"Yeah, that's what's so wonderful about it."

Dolly stood up. "I'd ask you to join our club, but once you get a date with Travis Cameo, you're disqualified. We all hope to be disqualified soon. We're hoping our club will self-destruct through total success. We'd all love to be in your shoes. That includes me. You really did it."

Dolly walked to the front door. She shook my hand, as if to confirm that she had come on official business. "I'm the treasurer of the club," she said. "Did I mention that?"

"I can't remember."

"We collected money to buy a rosebush to plant in my backyard. We call it the Travis Rose."

"May it thrive," I said as I showed her out the door.

She started down the steps, and then turned back. "Can I have your autograph?"

"Why?"

"Because you went out with Travis Cameo."

I shook my head no and closed the door.

Hero worship! But where was the hero? Just because a guy has mass appeal. Dumb. I wondered if Travis considered *me* as one of his fans. I had merely praised his horse picture. I wished someone would start a fan club for me. A dozen guys huddled together scheming to get a date with Jody Kline, enshrining lint from my sweater, and purchasing the most flourishing rosebush in the entire state of New York to grow the Jody Rose. No, that wasn't what I wanted. I didn't want the dozen guys. I only wanted one.

17

I was beginning to think there was a conspiracy between my mother and father to keep me from finding out what was happening between them. For me they were putting up a neutral, kind of bland front. Maybe they were saving their fights and other unpleasantness for the times when I wasn't around.

But one night, when I had just walked in after having supper at Alison's, I caught them in a fight. They were upstairs and I was downstairs, but I could hear them.

"Gerald, if you're not glad I came back, I'll leave."

"I'm glad. That much I've admitted to myself. But how glad and for how long, I don't know yet."

"I feel like I'm auditioning to be your wife again."

"Well, Sue, let's be frank. You already had the part and you walked out on it."

I didn't want to hear any more. It wasn't my business. Not exactly. And yet it was. Still, eavesdropping isn't my thing. I slipped back out the door. Sooner or later I'd learn the result of their fight.

Outside my house, I didn't know what to do. I couldn't just stand there. I could walk around the block and walk around the block and walk around the block. How long could a fight last? All night? I had homework to do.

I went back into the house and yelled, "I'm home. Any phone calls?"

That did it. They stopped. They were quiet. My father came downstairs.

"No calls," he said.

"Mom's upstairs?"

"Yes."

"I heard you two fighting."

"I'm sorry."

"Don't be. It was a sign of life. I want to know what's going on. I'm not a little kid who has to be protected. How'd you like to take a walk around the block?"

"I'll get my coat."

Outside, my father spoke first. "I know you're curious and impatient and I'd be, too, if I were in your place. I think I still love your mother. Or you might say I love her again. This isn't a fact, it's a possibility. Then there's that little matter of trust. I'm not sure about that, either. I'm beginning to understand why she did what she did. I'm beginning to feel comfortable with her in the house. What can I tell you? Love, trust, comfort. They're in what you might call an incipient stage."

We turned a corner. My father stopped walking. He asked, "Are *you* comfortable with her? I get the feeling that you are."

"We're getting along, Dad. Don't worry about Mom and me. I mean, I'm not going to pick out another mother. You're the one with the big decision to make. Like, what about Gossamer? She's really the one who should be impatient."

We started to walk again. My father chuckled slightly.

"Is Gossamer funny?" I asked.

"No, it's just that she's such a surprise. She was angry at first, but lately she's been remarkably understanding. I can't understand what's come over her, but I'm not complaining."

"I'm complaining about her son."

"There's nothing new?"

"Nope. You might say we're in a holding pattern."

"It's my fault."

"No, it isn't. I don't want you to rush into anything. I can see that you need time." I hesitated. Was this the moment to tell him about Uncle Mike? My father was putting as much emphasis on trust as he was on love. Would I be butting in or would I be doing the right thing? I didn't want to hurt him, but sooner or later he'd be hurt if my suspicions about Uncle Mike were on target.

We turned another corner. And I made a decision. I would talk to my mother about Uncle Mike.

"I love you, Dad," I said.

My father put his arm around me and we walked like that the rest of the way home.

18

I received a long letter from Opal.

Dear Jody,

This is in prompt response to both of your letters, although a bit more prompt in regard to the second letter, of course. I'm sorry about your problems, and I will plunge right into them. First, Matt Green. You are not presently in an action-type situation there. I know that this observation, coming from me, will surprise you, and you might think that Montana has dulled my senses. It hasn't. Sometimes the best action is inaction. I don't know if I made that up or read it somewhere, so I will not appropriate it as my own. I am still writing my "Fragments" and have an ever-growing collection.

Next, Uncle Mike. If my own mother were still living, I would not want her to get involved with anyone named Uncle Mike. I would cross the street to avoid such a person. However, as you point out, his name may not be Uncle Mike. In which case I certainly wouldn't want my mother to get involved with him. Yet, things are not always as they seem. I force myself to resort to this cliché expression because cliché expressions are ninety-five percent more accurate than most other expressions. You are going to need ingenuity to work this one out. And facts. You need more facts, dear Jody. If I were in New York, I would market-research Uncle Mike for you. But I'm afraid you're on your own. When you get the facts, send them to me. Then my opinion will be forthcoming. Is New York still there? It doesn't seem that way when you're living in Montana.

Love from your friend,
Opal O'Malley Spiegel Stamp

I wondered what Opal would say if she knew about the gray-blue car. I guess I had used ingenuity in advance of her telling me to. Her advice was okay, and she can't be blamed for her timing.

I owed it to Opal to keep up my ingenuity. I put on a jacket and walked over to Mrs. Ronstone's house. The car wasn't in front and wasn't in the driveway. I had checked on the car a few days earlier, and a few days before that. This was the third time in a row that the car wasn't there. Had Uncle Mike moved?

I kept walking. I felt that I was at a dead end. There was something about the empty driveway, something that said, "Sorry, kid, this was your last clue and you didn't do anything about it. Do you think clues are a dime a dozen?"

When I finally returned to my house, my mother was entertaining. Yes, entertaining. Her old friends had flocked back and she was picking up some new ones. I wanted to caution her about the new friends, but I let it go. I was sure my mother was known as the woman who skipped out on her husband and daughter for two years. If she had left my father and divorced him, well, that was kind of ordinary. But to leave, travel all over the world, and then come back to live in the house, that was something else. It's easy to become a celebrity in modern society. If you achieve any kind of notoriety, its inevitable by-product is that you become a star. Except for some clucking busybodies who always peered out self-righteously behind their trimmed hedges and were throwbacks to a more strict era, the town regarded my mother with awe and admiration. I had been so afraid they would shun her, and yet it bothered me now that they embraced her like a woman of accomplishment. She had joined several clubs and was chairperson of two committees. On the home front she was buying new furniture for the house.

I nodded to the women and went upstairs. My mother was definitely reestablished in the community, in her house, and, with a little luck and help from Uncle Mike, with my father. It was probably going just as she had planned. But I was about to wreck her plans.

I waited until my mother's friends had left. Then I went downstairs. "Let's talk," I said solemnly as my mother piled up coffee cups.

"Sure," she said, and she sat down in a chair she was soon to replace. "What about?"

"Uncle Mike."

"Uncle Mike? You're kidding. What is there to talk about?"

"Dad doesn't like him. He doesn't want him in the house."

"I know. I had to start meeting Uncle Mike on the outside."

"That sounds pretty sordid."

"Is this some kind of joke? I'm not interested in Uncle Mike as a *man*. He's been a friend and a kind of financial adviser. I have a trust fund, something independent from your father. That's what enabled me to travel. But the trust fund has been a burden, too. I hate handling money, and Uncle Mike tried to help. Well, it doesn't matter anymore. Your father must have scared him off, because I haven't heard from him in over a week. I guess your father was jealous of him. I think that's so cute and touching."

"*Cute? Touching?* What kind of game are you playing?"

My mother sighed. "Jody, I realize that it's going to take time for us to get back to the way we were. Maybe we can never get back completely. Everything is a bit awkward. But aren't you taking Uncle Mike too seriously?"

I started to walk out of the room. "You're a very clever human being," I said, "and I hope my father marries Gossamer Green."

19

Dolly Bergstater wanted to be my friend. I was far below Travis Cameo on the Worship Scale, but I was some sort of idol to her. My date with Travis had enhanced me in the eyes of many of the girls at school. It reminded me of my mother's newly elevated status. Fame in the fast lane. Not earned, just heaped on you.

Dolly was only thirteen. I was a fifteen-year-old junior. That had something to do with her wonderful opinion of me. But she thought I was better than she was. *That* bothered me. She was trying to buy my friendship by handing out bits of information about Travis. It wasn't a bribery kind of thing. It was just an attempt to be worthy of my attention and time.

Dolly's the one who told me that Travis had the flu.

"One hundred and two degrees," she said as she

walked into my house one day. "If he hasn't contacted you again, that's why."

I didn't want to let on that this was really useful
information. Travis had hinted that he'd get in touch
with me. I didn't see him at school the week after our
date, but that didn't mean anything. Sometimes I'd
happen to see him at school, and sometimes I
wouldn't. But if he was out with the flu, that explained why he hadn't called. Then again, maybe it
didn't necessarily explain anything. Travis could
have been in rousing good health and still not called.
Now I wouldn't know how I stood with him until his
temperature went down.

I invited Dolly up to my room. It was private. We
could talk there. "Dolly," I said, "it's none of my
business, but I think you should get yourself a different hobby. Replace Travis with woodworking or
something."

"Where's the sex appeal in woodworking?" Dolly
asked.

"You'd be doing something that belongs to *you*.
What you're doing right now is futile. You're a bunch
of freshman girls, right?"

Dolly nodded.

"And you've latched on to this senior or this image
of a senior, and you've lost sight of yourselves. Did
you ever think that *you* might be as interesting as he
is?"

"I've assessed myself and found myself wanting,"
said Dolly. "Fact is, I'm extraordinarily dull."

"No, you're *not,* Dolly. You're kind of quirky, and that in itself is interesting."

"You think so?"

"Sure. Why don't you just disband this club and concentrate on yourself. Go out and buy a Dolly Rose. Put a blowup of your own picture on the wall."

"It wouldn't be the same," said Dolly. "It couldn't match the dramatic futility of yearning for someone who doesn't know you exist. And the challenge of changing that. The challenge of the dream."

Instead of woodworking, Dolly might have found a fine outlet in political speechmaking. She was qualified. She didn't know what she was talking about, but she made it sound pretty good.

"Are you my friend?" she asked suddenly. "Like, if I tell people you're my friend, will you back me up?"

"I'm your friend," I said.

"My best friend?"

"Dolly, we hardly know each other. And anyway, Alison August has been my best friend for years. But you and I can still be friends."

"Has Alison ever been out with Travis? If so, our club doesn't have that information."

"Alison has been going out with Pete Summers practically since the day of her birth."

"Seriously?"

"She's never dated anyone else."

"If I could go out with Travis Cameo, I'd never date anyone else."

"Oh c'mon. You're only thirteen. You're entitled to some variety."

"I'd wash his clothes, I'd sweep his floors, I'd be his slave."

Poor Dolly. She was so eager, so unformed, so *starting out*. She had a lot to learn. She probably would have camped out at my house if she'd known about the phone call I would receive a few days later. Travis phoned. "I've been sick," he said. "That's why I didn't call sooner."

"I heard you were sick. Feeling better?"

"Kind of. This thing leaves you a little weak. But I had to call to say I'll call you just as soon as I'm back to normal."

Travis had redeemed himself. He wasn't a make-out artist like Duane after all. He wanted to take me out again even though I'd rebuffed him in the car. I had been wrong about him.

"Well, then, a very speedy recovery," I said.

"Thanks. I'm not contagious anymore, but the doctor thinks I'd better stay home from school a few more days and get my rest, as he puts it. So I'm nursing my beet-red nose, watery eyes, and I'm driving my mother crazy."

"I can't picture you with a beet-red nose and watery eyes."

"I look like your basic disaster area."

"Yuh, well, if you say so."

There really wasn't anything else to say over the phone. Phone conversations have a rhythm, and when you sense the rhythm is running out, that's the time to say good-bye. I should have said good-bye right then. But I didn't. I said, "How would you like a surprise to cheer you up?"

"Anything is better than watching game shows and soap operas on TV. Don't spoil the surprise, but give me a hint what it is."

"Delivery service. That's the hint. Maybe even this afternoon if I can arrange it. Are you decent? I mean, can someone from the outside world visit you?"

"If they can get past my mother and if they can stand seeing me in my present condition, which also includes a grungy bathrobe. Are you the delivery service?"

"No. I'm just the girl you're going to phone as soon as you're all better."

"Sounds good to me. Good-bye, Jody."

"Good-bye, Travis."

20

Dolly screamed when I told her what I had in mind.

"Go over there? On the hallowed grounds of his home? In person? With a bouquet of roses?"

"Yes. Finally you can *meet* Travis and rid yourself of this fixation."

"But Jody, this will nourish my fixation."

"I don't think so."

Travis had, according to his own description, a beet-red nose, watery eyes, a grungy bathrobe, adding up to "your basic disaster area." Perfect. Dolly would be disillusioned when she saw him. She would see firsthand what some people don't get to see until they've been married a few years: the object of their affections at his or her very worst. She would be free.

"Jody, I can't walk into his house with flowers. Anyway, my roses are dead. That is, they're not roses yet.

This isn't their season. I have a bush with a beautiful future, but right now it's just a bush."

"So take part of the bush. You can say it's from me. I told him to expect a delivery. It's a perfect excuse and I set it up for you. His mother's home, so you don't have to worry about being alone with him."

"That would never worry me."

I began to wonder if anything would discourage Dolly's devotion to Travis. What if she didn't simply deliver the bush, see him at his worst, and leave? The beet-red nose, the watery eyes, the grungy bathrobe, might bring out the Florence Nightingale in her. She, an angel in white, would hover over Travis Cameo, rescuing him from the jaws of death, according to the report she would give her fan club. She might pester him, beg to scrub his toilet, fluff his pillows, massage his feet, and he'd blame me for it.

"You know something, Dolly," I said, "you're right. You've got a dead-looking bush, and in general the idea stinks."

"I told you it did."

Once again, a telephone conversation was running down, and I didn't let it run out. I had to add something. A lie. "Besides," I said, "he's contagious."

"Contagious?"

"Very."

"Oh, thanks for telling me. Bye."

"Bye."

I was relieved. I had gotten in and out of something sticky. At least that's what I thought at the time. No one had told me that catching a disease from the one you love—having something physical transmitted from his body to yours, even accompanied by a red nose and watery eyes—is considered in some circles as the highest form of eroticism.

I learned too late that shortly after my telephone call to Dolly Bergstater, she had set out from her house, a scraggly rosebush with unborn roses in her hand, absolutely determined to catch Travis Cameo's flu.

21

Travis was back in school. I saw him walking into assembly. But I didn't stop him. He was supposed to call me. I was waiting for that. I didn't know what day he returned to school. My major source of Travis information was home sick. I found that out when I called Dolly's house after not hearing from her for several days.

I decided to visit Dolly after she had been absent from school for a week. Her father had assured me over the phone that she wasn't contagious. On the way to her house, I walked by Mrs. Ronstone's house. I was still doing that even though I hadn't seen the car parked in her driveway for several weeks.

Mrs. Ronstone was outside her house with Poopsie. I was surprised. I had never seen her outside, and I figured Poopsie never got walked. Maybe that accounted for his sour disposition.

"Hello, Mrs. Ronstone."

She didn't recognize me.

"I'm the friend of the artist who's drawing Poopsie's portrait," I said. "I was with him the afternoon you were arranging for the picture."

"Oh, yes," said Mrs. Ronstone. "I recall that. I'm afraid your friend's been sick with the flu and had to stop midway in the picture. But now he's back working on it."

"In good health, fit and able?" I asked.

"Good as new."

I already knew that, but I just wanted to make sure. I had seen Travis walking into assembly, good as new. He was definitely able to go out on a date.

Mrs. Ronstone and Poopsie started to walk along with me. Maybe Mrs. Ronstone could tell me something I *didn't* already know. Opal Stamp, it's ingenuity time for Jody Kline again.

I said to Mrs. Ronstone, "I'm sorry I disturbed your boarder that time."

Mrs. Ronstone stopped. "You disturbed my boarder? Oh, you mean Rita?"

"Rita?"

"Rita's my boarder. I rent spare rooms. Don't tell the neighbors. They don't want any commerce in the neighborhood."

"The boarder I disturbed was a man. He wore crew socks and sneakers."

"My, aren't you the observant one. I suspected that the man never changed his socks."

"Is he still with you?"

"No. He wasn't with me very long."

"How long?"

"Why do you want to know?" Mrs. Ronstone was getting suspicious. "Do you know him?"

"I heard someone call him Uncle Mike."

"Oh, well, whatever they want to call him." She started to walk again. She didn't want to talk about her boarders. It was maddening. Locked up in her head was information I needed badly. But she was back to dogs. "Does your artist friend do dachshunds? I have a friend who might be interested."

"I think so," I said. "Anything with a tail. Well, it was nice seeing you, Mrs. Ronstone."

"Yes, lovely," she said.

I walked ahead. So, Uncle Mike had moved out. My mother had said she wasn't seeing him anymore. Was there a connection between his moving out and my mother not seeing him? Why speculate. The guy had accomplished his purpose. Things were going very harmoniously at the residence of Mr. and Mrs. Gerald Kline these days, and that was very much to Mrs. Kline's advantage. She was still occupying the guest room, but time and this continuing harmony would probably take care of that. She was also treating me as if I hadn't blown up at her, hadn't made accusations about her and Uncle Mike. Either it hadn't registered or she expected friction between us and this was just part of the expected friction. Matt hadn't called me. That was probably my fault. He wanted to keep in touch. But the harmony between my parents was continuing bad news for Matt and his mother. And by extension, between Matt and me.

At Dolly's house, Mr. Bergstater showed me up to her room. Then he closed the door so we could be alone. He was a quiet and lovable man. He had ways about him that reminded me of Dolly, although she wasn't quiet. I didn't see a mother around. Dolly had never mentioned one. This was my first time in her house.

She was sitting up in bed, and she looked better sick than well. She was surrounded by papers, and she was smiling. "Hi," she said.

"Hi. How do you feel?"

"Fine. I'm going back to school on Monday."

"Great. What are all those papers? Catching up on your homework?"

"No. I'm forming a Rodney Smash Fan Club. He's hot in the international music scene."

"Really? Is that in addition to your other fan club?"

"It's a replacement for my other fan club."

"What about being able to pick lint off of Rodney's sweater?"

"Not important. In fact, distance and space are necessary to keep a fan club going. There should be thousands of miles between fans and subject."

"That isn't the way you used to talk. Dolly, something has happened. Did you go over to Travis's house? How did you get the flu?"

"Okay. How did I get the flu? I don't have the flu. I have a sprained ankle. *Had.* It's okay now."

"So you didn't go over to Travis's house? Good."

"I went over. That's how I got my sprained ankle. Fleeing."

"Fleeing?"

"Yeah, the guy makes Duane Rabinowitz look like a quivering sheep. I mean, there he was sick in bed and looking so washed-out that your stomach would turn. Well, I was nice to him because basically I'm an empathic person and he was a sick person. I gave him the rosebush branches, I offered to get him a glass of water, I smoothed his blankets. The last was a mistake. He lunged at me. And with his mother just downstairs, too. He tried to take advantage of me because I'm not an experienced woman. Boy, was that a turn-off for me. Listen, tarnished heroes are like scum. I'm not talking warts. I'm not talking pimples. I'm talking *tarnish*. Well, I got out of there as fast as I could, which resulted in this sprained ankle."

"Oh boy."

"When you were out with him, did he try anything?"

"He might have been in the process. He might not have. I wasn't sure."

"I'm sure. And I wasn't there. I can't understand how a person who goes around painting dogs' pictures could be so unsavory. And a class officer, too. If I had credentials like his, I'd try to live up to them. Anyway, I reported back to the club, we voted to disband immediately. Say, are you still my friend? You didn't want me to visit him."

"Of course I'm still your friend."

"How about Travis Cameo? Are you still his friend?"

"If I could give him back the flu, I would. Does that answer your question?"

On the way home I realized that Dolly had thoroughly carried out her mission to find out whatever there was to find out about Travis Cameo. In a way, she had done my work for me. Travis probably wouldn't call me. He had called me when he was sick because sick people get itchy for diversion, for any break in the routine.

I was revolted by his trying to take advantage of Dolly. It was my fault that Dolly had gone over there. I wanted to tell him off. But some people aren't worthy of your anger. They are worthy of your indifference.

22

It was hard to be indifferent toward Travis Cameo. I hardly ever saw him at school. And how do you effectively show indifference? "Hi there, Travis. I'm indifferent toward you. Have you noticed? Pay attention to my indifference!"

Indifference was not satisfying. And whenever I saw Dolly, I felt that I owed her something. I started to look for Travis. One day I saw him just outside of school. I went up to him. "Hello, Travis."

"Hi, Jody. How've you been?"

"So-so. I see you're over the flu."

"Fully recovered except for the doctor's bills."

Travis laughed. His laugh, which I used to find appealing, was now annoying.

"Travis, a friend of mine visited you while you were sick and brought you a gift. Some, uh, future flowers."

"Oh, sure. The fan-club kid."

"You know about the fan club?"

"Of course. Something like that gets around."

"She said you tried to grab her."

Travis scratched his head. "Grab her?"

"Lunge at her. Whatever."

Travis raised his hand. "Stop. I know what you mean. I guess *she* didn't know what I meant. Hasn't anyone ever given her a harmless hug?"

"A *hug?*"

"Yeah. She was kind of sweet, and I like sweet girls. I mean, they don't have to be sweet, but it's a nice quality. My hug was like a thank-you for her coming over."

"You scared her out of her skull."

"Me? I'm not scary. I just like girls."

I gave him a cold look.

He shifted from one foot to the other. "Jody, remember when I met you in the park and I said my name was Picasso? I was only half kidding. Picasso had plenty of girl friends, he liked women, and I don't consider myself a slouch in that department either. Maybe it goes with the territory of being an artist."

I felt like retorting that I was an artist and it didn't go with my territory. But I didn't. There was something familiar about this conversation. As if I'd had it before. In a way, I had. It reminded me of talks with my mother. My mother had also tried to define herself. This is me, and this is the way I am. Define yourself and you can do whatever you want. You're entitled to forgiveness.

Still, what was there to forgive Travis for? He had said he'd call me again, but he hadn't. It wasn't exactly a crime. He was simply a guy who liked girls, girls, girls. And they liked him back. Maybe it was hard for him to keep track of his phone calls.

But I'd have to set Dolly straight. I'd have to tell her that what she was now describing as "a major kind of lunge" had been meant as a friendly hug.

"Can we be friends? Maybe go out sometime? Talk about things? Paint together?"

Travis was talking to me. He meant it and he didn't mean it. Right now he meant it, but tomorrow he might be off in another direction. I was about to tell him that yes, we could be friends, when I saw Dolly coming toward us. She looked angry. When she got close, I reached out and tugged at her arm. "Dolly, got a moment?"

"In a minute," she said.

"Now is better, Dolly. It really is."

"You don't have to fight my battles for me, Jody. I can do this myself."

Dolly turned to Travis. "You are an unmitigated crumb. Next to you, Duane Rabinowitz is a gem. He's up front, and totally honest in his sliminess. He wears his repulsiveness with a beautiful frankness and insincerity that is rare in today's slick society. You can't hold a candle to Rabinowitz."

Travis was speechless.

Dolly pulled me away. "Were you trying to tell Travis off for me?" she asked.

"Well, yes. But you see, it's not—"

"I can do that for myself. I had planned to do it. Just because I'm a scrawny freshman girl with some airhead ideas doesn't mean I have to be protected. I got a bigger high from telling off that guy than I ever got from the touching, the lint-picking, the gazing at the photo. Because it was *me* as a person doing something, not me as a stupid fan. Know what I mean? That's what you were always trying to tell me, wasn't it?"

"Something like that."

"And you were out there trying to fight my battle because you're bigger and older and levelheaded. You don't have to be maternalistic. I don't have a mother, but I get along. You underestimated me. Scrawny, frizzy-haired, motherless girls are always in danger of being underestimated."

"Not anymore. Not by me."

"Good. That only leaves the rest of society. I can handle it."

"I was motherless for two years. My mother went away, but now she's back." I felt like telling her.

"I'm glad for you. My mother's really gone."

I didn't want to ask if she was dead or what.

Dolly didn't want to talk about it. She said, "You're a friend. Some friends never get a chance to pass the test of friendship, but you did. Am I your best friend in the thirteen-year-old category?"

"Sure."

"Why did you tug at my arm before? Got something to tell me?"

"I did. But the moment has passed. It has definitely passed."

23

It was Thanksgiving. My mother and Betty prepared our meal. Then Betty went home to spend the holiday with her own family.

My mother got dressed up in a red dress, and she and my father and I sat around the dining room table eating an absolutely traditional meal, as if we were an absolutely traditional family. My father carved the turkey. Husband, father, attorney, solid member of the community—it was all being reaffirmed on this Thanksgiving Day.

I wondered how Gossamer Green was spending the day. Perhaps she and my father had a plan to spend Thanksgiving evening together. Perhaps, at Gossamer's place, there was yet another turkey waiting to be carved, another meal waiting to be eaten.

The telephone rang. "I'll get it," I said. I went to the den and picked up the telephone.

"Jody?"

It was Matt!

I played it cool. "Hi, Matt. Happy Thanksgiving."

I was elated that he was thinking of me on the holiday. Holidays have a way of breaking down practical decisions, stern resolve, and all things sensible. Sentiment prevails.

"Jody, I didn't call about Thanksgiving."

Sentiment keels over and dies.

"Is there something wrong? You sound terrible. Is anybody dead?"

"Only a relationship. I have news."

"Whose relationship? What kind of news?"

Here it comes. Matt and I were really finished. But calling about it on Thanksgiving Day wasn't my idea of thoughtful timing.

"You'll be shocked, Jody."

"I'm more shocked not knowing. Tell me before I split!"

"My mother and father remarried."

"What?"

"My mother and father remarried."

"How did it happen? Why did it happen?"

"It's no great mystery. Your father's been spending less and less time with my mother. Thanksgiving was the last straw. Your father elected to spend it with your mother. It's much better this way. My parents will be happy and your parents will be happy."

"My father doesn't know about this? I mean, your mother didn't give him a warning or a clue?"

"No. She just went out, bought a new outfit, and eloped."

My poor father. Now he had no one. That is, he had no one who deserved him. I should have told him about Uncle Mike the minute I saw that man at Mrs. Ronstone's house. I should have told my father that he was the victim of some kind of conspiracy dreamed up by my mother. My father would have once and for all rejected my mother. And settled for Gossamer.

Gossamer Green. Mostly I had viewed her as a woman who would change the color of her nail polish five times a day if it didn't harm her nails. Polishing her nails was the definitive act of her life. Hairdressers, clothing designers, and astrologists thrive on people like her. But she had made my father happy in an unhappy period. And now, compared to my mother, Gossamer seemed pure and untainted.

"Jody, are you still there?"

"Still here."

"It's good to be talking to you again, Jody. Can I see you?"

"When?"

"Anytime you say."

"I have to let everything sink in. I don't know how I feel about anybody or anything."

"Does that include me?"

"Maybe. Everything's set for you now. Your parents are back together. It's nice and neat. But I'm left with a situation I have to deal with. You can't just walk back into my life because *your* life is okay."

"I understand. I'd feel the same way if I were in your shoes. Take your time. I'll call again. And I know this will sound terrible to you, but happy Thanksgiving, Jody."

"Not this one. Maybe next year. Bye, Matt."

I went back to my parents, who hadn't heard any of the conversation.

"Who was that?" my father asked as he spooned some cranberry sauce onto his plate.

"Matt Green."

"He called to wish you a happy Thanksgiving Day. Fine! That's a nice gesture."

My father, getting too full of stuffing, sweet potato, and other satisfying stuff, forgot he was a lawyer who was not supposed to draw conclusions without facts to substantiate them. But I didn't say anything. I sat there, gazing at my mother and father, and thinking, I know something you don't know . . . I know something you don't know. It was like the chant of diabolical schoolchildren, and it went around and around in my head.

In due course we got to the pumpkin pie and tea. We were near the end of the meal. I had to tell them the news sometime. Quite soon my dear mother would know she really did have something to be thankful for on this special day.

I was loading dishes and utensils into the dishwasher. I felt that the sacred part of the day, the part that shouldn't be broken into or chipped or defiled, was over. We had eaten. We had been made aware of thankfulness and good fortune. My parents were sitting there, relaxed and full.

I went back to the table and sat down. "Matt called with some news," I said. "Something exciting."

"Oh?" My mother lifted her eyebrows, mother-style, as she waited to hear that Matt had invited me to a prom. What prom, it didn't matter. It was the consummate invitation, beloved by mothers of daughters. And my mother, having missed out on two years of happy teen-age-type news, was poised to participate in shared squeals of delight.

I might never in my life have another chance to drop a bomb. But I was sorry I had to drop this one.

"Matt's mother and father remarried," I said.

"What?"

"Huh?"

My father said *what* and my mother said *huh*. I repeated, "Matt's mother and father remarried. I forgot to ask when it happened. Today, I think."

My father was stunned. "How could she do that? Just up and do that? She never gave me a hint. . . ."

"Maybe she did and you didn't notice, Dad. Or maybe you were giving her hints and *you* didn't notice. Things couldn't go on the way they were."

"Excuse me." My father got up and left the room. I think he went to call Matt to verify the information.

I turned to my mother "So, Mom, he's all yours. On a platter on this most appropriate of all days. Feast on your victory."

"Jody! I've never met this woman. Her remarriage has nothing to do with me. Your father could have moved out of the house. He could have divorced me and married her. If some woman I've never met wants to get married, or remarried, *whatever,* don't you dare blame me!"

My mother swept out of the room. I would never forget the events of this Thanksgiving Day. To the outside world, it probably would sound perfect. My mother and father together without another woman in the picture. Matt's mother and father together without another man in the picture. It should have come out smooth and even. But it didn't.

24

Dolly got herself a new hairdo. I didn't think it was an improvement over her old hairdo, but it was the idea that counted. A new hairdo is supposed to be a sign of burgeoning feelings of self-esteem. She wasn't going to be anybody's slave from now on.

The time I was spending with Dolly cut into the time I usually spent with Alison. It took me an hour to bring Alison up-to-date on my parents and Matt. She didn't know what to say about my parents. But she had plenty to say about Matt. "Matt's easy," said Alison. "He wants to see you. He *cares,* Jody. He always has. He was mature enough to step back when he saw that his feelings about his mother were affecting his relationship with you. Can't you see that?"

"I can see it. But his problems with his mother are solved. And my problems with my mother are unsolved."

"Why don't you have a talk with her?"

"I did, remember? I told her I hoped Dad would marry Gossamer."

"Right. Well, how about talking to your Dad?"

"And spilling the beans about Uncle Mike? I can't hurt him."

"You're a mess. Why don't you paint a thousand pictures? It'll take your mind off your family."

"I'll think about it," I said.

"No, you won't," said Alison.

Alison was right. I couldn't think about pictures. I just went along from day to day. Surprisingly, my marks at school were terrific, and a couple of teachers complimented me on my attention in the classroom. My energies had to go somewhere, and I guess they went into my schoolwork.

I received a postcard from Opal with this message: NEWS, PLEASE.

One morning at breakfast, while my mother was still asleep, my father asked if I could go into the city someday and meet him for dinner, just the two of us.

"Sure. Tomorrow would be good for me. I have a short day at school."

"Fine."

"Dad, is this about anything special?"

"Yes."

The next afternoon I took the commuter train into New York City. I walked the few blocks from Grand Central Station to the building where my father's law office is located. The firm just took in their twenty-fourth lawyer.

Mrs. Baxter presides over the reception area and she's been doing it for about twenty years. Her image specialty is professional competence and imperturbability, which is supposed to be a preview of the professional competence and imperturbability you'll find when you have your appointment with one of the lawyers inside. She usually dresses in black or dark blue, as if she's intent upon imposing a certain respectability and drabness on the viewer.

"Your father is expecting you," she said to me, and she motioned that I could proceed inside. The walk down the wide hall to my father's office was a journey through intrigue. Behind the closed doors that lined the hall, the ways in which we bruise one another or seek justice or revenge or merely a fair deal or a financially favorable way to die were being coolly discussed over luxurious velvet carpeting at enormous hourly fees by lawyers who gave the impression that they themselves were immune to life's problems. Their roofs never leaked, their shirts never got lost at the laundry, and their wives never skipped out on them for two years.

I didn't see Matt. Usually he's up and down the halls, doing things for various lawyers. But now that he was a student at Columbia, he put in fewer hours at the firm. Anyway, I didn't have to run into him in order to see him. He *wanted* to see me. He had told me that. I wanted to see him, too. But I needed to feel right about everything, about inviting him into my house, about being the daughter of Mr. and Mrs. Gerald Kline.

My father was working on some papers. When he saw me, he stood up and said, "It's only four thirty, a bit early for dinner, but let's go anyway." Then he kissed me hello as we walked out of the office.

We went to a restaurant that he had taken me to several times before. This was a quiet period and the waiter gave us prompt attention. We ordered quickly. Then my father looked at me across the table and I almost felt like I was a client back at the law firm having a consultation in one of those closed-door rooms. Then again, maybe I wasn't a client. Maybe I was an adversary.

"Dad," I said, "I'll make it easy for you. You're going to tell me that you and Mom are resuming your marriage or you're going to tell me that you're leaving the house or you're going to tell me that you're trying to get Mom out of the house. One of the above."

My father smiled. "You're right. One of the above. Jody, here it is. Remember our around-the-block walk and talk? I was still unsure of my feelings. Well, now I'm not. I really *love* your mother. Gossamer figured it out before I did. Maybe she's smarter than I am. At any rate, I haven't told your mother yet because I want your approval, your blessing. . . ."

"My approval? My blessing? You love Mom and you're going to tell her if you get my permission?"

"Not your permission. But I'd like your approval."

"You forgave her for the two years?"

"I didn't forgive. I'm accepting her as she is."

"I'm not. She's been deceiving you."

"Deceiving me? No, she's not like that. Whatever she's done has been out in the open. Where did you get an idea like that?"

"Never mind. I know what I'm talking about."

My father leaned toward me. "What *are* you talking about?"

"I'm talking about how she tried to make you jealous with Uncle Mike."

My father's expression changed when I mentioned Uncle Mike.

I went on. "I can tell by looking at you right now that her Uncle Mike plan worked."

"It didn't, Jody. Let's drop it."

"I can't! See, it was . . . well, what would you call it in law . . . fraud? Uncle Mike wasn't any big-shot fitness executive."

I could see that my father was upset. "How do you know that?" he asked.

"I know because I happened to be at a Mrs. Ronstone's house one day. She lives a few blocks from us. I saw Uncle Mike there and Mrs. Ronstone said he was her boarder. But Uncle Mike had told me he lived in a skyscraper in New York City. I know that rich people sometimes have second homes, but it wouldn't be a spare room at Mrs. Ronstone's."

I stopped. I wanted this to register with my father. He often complained about lawyers who orate fable into fact. But my story was true, and it was registering. So I went on.

"Mom told me that she met Uncle Mike in London and how successful he was. I don't know where or how she actually met him, but they cooked up all this success stuff to make you jealous, to make you think you had a powerful rival for Mom. And it worked."

"It didn't work. I told you it didn't work, Jody."

"Okay, let's say it didn't work. What do you think of Mom now?"

"I think she's sweet and dear. That's what I thought when I married her. Her flaws emerged in rather rapid succession, but I imagine that mine did, too."

"That's it? A few rapidly emerging flaws? After what I just told you? That's the worst you can say about her?"

My father frowned. "I wish you could forget Uncle Mike, but I see that you can't. And I can't have you thinking these awful things about your mother."

Our dinners came, but my father looked at his as if he were waiting for the waiter to clear it away. I couldn't touch mine, either.

"Jody," my father said, "I had no idea *you* knew about Uncle Mike. I knew you met him, but I thought that was it. You see, Jody, I've known almost from the start that he wasn't Uncle Mike."

I had a dozen questions. But I let my father keep on talking.

"This is going to be a shocker for you, Jody. The only person who didn't know that Uncle Mike was a phony was your mother!"

"*She* didn't know? *You* knew?"

"Yes. Your mother did meet him in London. She met him as Uncle Mike. That's not his real name or his real nickname. He made it up. This Uncle Mike is . . . *was* . . . a private detective. I employed him, through a reputable agency, to check up on your mother. I was thinking about divorcing her. She was flitting around. Here, there. For all I knew, she had taken up with another man and had no intention of ever returning. In her own fashion she'd get around to telling me, I was sure, but I was disgusted with her calling the shots. I felt justified in doing things my own way. The detective agency used a Talbot Jones, one of their highly experienced employees, to do some discreet checking. That's all. Unfortunately he concluded that your mother was loaded with money and that some of it should be his. That's when Uncle Mike was born. Instead of watching your mother, he introduced himself as this highly successful business-man. He reasoned that it's easier to get money from someone who thinks you have plenty yourself."

"Pretty smooth."

"That's his business. His real business. He's sup-posed to be clever, imaginative, devious, stealthy, and a chameleon of sorts. A good private detective has to be multitalented."

"And honest."

My father actually smiled. "Yeah, honest. If he had been honest, I wouldn't be telling you about him."

"Okay, so he introduced himself to Mom as Uncle Mike in London. Then what?"

"London turned out to be your mother's last stop before she came home. Uncle Mike followed her here, took up residence in the neighborhood, and

pretended he was working in his so-called office in
New York City and living in an apartment house
there. Meanwhile he was trying to get your mother
to invest in some phony companies."

"But he took a chance moving into the area. If he's
so smart, why did he take a chance like that?"

"First of all, this was a short-term operation. He
wasn't planning to stick around very long. Also, Mrs.
Ronstone didn't want the neighbors to know she was
taking in boarders. Uncle Mike must have answered
an ad. I'm not sure about that. At any rate, her desire
for secrecy and his desire for secrecy meshed. Her
place was cheap, convenient, but most of all, appealing in its audacity. He must have chuckled every
time he made the short drive from his place to ours."

My father spoke faster. "I followed him home
once. Your mother had invited him over just to drop
off some papers. Then I followed him."

"What about the first time you met him?"

"Of course I didn't *know* who this Uncle Mike was
the first time he showed up at our house. But I didn't
trust him, especially when your mother mentioned
that she'd met him in London. I contacted the detective agency, they put two and two together—which
is their line of work, of course—and told me they
would take care of the matter promptly, and that this
man would never bother our family again. I guess
they took care of the matter. Uncle Mike disap-
peared."

"Then Mom doesn't know *any* of this?"

"She only knows that Uncle Mike, her financial counselor, has dropped out of her life."

"So she didn't know anything, but *you* did!"

"I'm the villain."

"No, you had a right to check up on her. But I wish you had told me. When I think of what I said to her . . . I had a fight with her over Uncle Mike."

"She never mentioned it. Sorry, Jody. When I get home, I'm going to tell her everything. I didn't think I'd ever have to, but it's better to start with a clean slate."

"Starting again, huh?"

"Yes. That was supposed to be the reason for this talk."

"Yeah, we in our ultimate wisdom were supposed to agree to take Mom back."

My father and I began to eat our dinners. "I have a question," I said.

"I know what it is," said my father. "After I talk to your mother, do you suppose she'll take *us* back?"

"The thought crossed my mind."

25

Blame. Once a person does something you don't approve of, something that may in fact be wrong, it's easy to blame other things on the same person. Just ask my mother. She could tell you plenty about that. My father had sent a private detective after her. I had created a conspiracy with her at the core. But that night when my father told my mother what he had done, she told him she would have been disappointed in him if he *hadn't* hired someone to check up on her. One of the things she loved about my father, she said, was his "excruciating caution." As for Uncle Mike, she dismissed him by saying his investment advice was "sprouting holes."

I wasn't there while my father slid neatly back into my mother's life. I had told him on the way home from our partially eaten dinner that his official recon-

ciliation with her shouldn't be a three-person deal.
He agreed.

I went to my room when we got home. The next
morning I got his report. We were both up early. My
mother was still upstairs. My mother isn't a breakfast
person. That's one of the things I had forgotten about
her. My father gave me his good news over hot ce-
real. It was better than the meal the night before.

Then he went off to work. I went off to school. In
the afternoon I would talk to my mother. It was my
turn. My father had successfully reunited with my
mother. I was next in line. Of course, if my mother's
committees or her old friends or her new friends
were at the house when I got home, I would have to
wait until the next day. Or the day after. What would
I say? "About my conspiracy theory, Mom, well it was
just a little error in judgment. Nothing serious. I just
didn't trust my own mother."

I walked to school with Alison. She wanted to know
more than I was willing to tell her about my parents.
I had decided that it was my father's private business
about hiring a detective. This meant that Alison
would never know the true story about Uncle Mike.
All I could tell her was that I had made a mistake, and
that my parents had reconciled and that I couldn't
give her the details.

"I would if I could," I said.

"I'll be waiting in case you weaken," she promised.
"And if it happens during this walk to school, so
much the better."

Dolly came up to us as soon as we got to school.

"Have you two ever met?" I asked.

"So you're my competition," Dolly said to Alison.

"For what?" asked Alison.

"Nothing," I said. "Dolly meet Alison. Alison meet Dolly."

Alison was staring at Dolly and Dolly was staring over Alison's shoulder. Travis Cameo was a few feet behind Alison.

"There he is," Dolly said to me. "I feel invigorated every time I see him. I'm alive with a renewed sense of ill will."

Now the three of us were watching Travis. He saw us. I thought he would turn away, but he came over!

"How are you?" he asked all of us, but his eyes were on Dolly.

I couldn't believe it.

"I am fine," Dolly said with great dignity.

"Have a good day," said Travis. He nodded to all of us, and walked on.

"What was that all about?" I asked Dolly.

"Well, his fury has subsided. He was furious at me after I told him off. Now his subsiding fury has turned into a quest for approval. Mine."

"Why should he need your approval?" asked Alison.

"Because he doesn't have it. All he has is the admiration of the entire senior class and most of the school. He has a greedy ego, and I'm wallowing in its need."

Alison looked extremely puzzled. Dolly has that effect on people. It was easy to underestimate Dolly, just as it was easy to overestimate Travis Cameo. This respective underestimation and overestimation would probably follow them all through their lives. In time, Dolly would learn to capitalize on it nicely, and Travis would learn that it couldn't get him everything he wanted. I had a hunch they were going to do some of this learning together.

Alison was still analyzing what Dolly had said. "Tell me about it," she said. "Make me understand it."

"Okay. Come over my house this afternoon. You too, Jody."

"I can't," I said. "I have something to do. But you two go ahead."

"I'll meet you here after the last class," Dolly said to Alison.

Alison, cheated out of the details on Uncle Mike and my parents, had to look elsewhere for excitement. I was glad that she and Dolly were hitting it off. I would have preferred going to Dolly's house after school. But I had to go home and face my mother.

After school I walked home by myself, and hoped to see numerous cars parked in front of my house when I got there. Even one visitor would be enough to postpone the talk with my mother. Maybe my mother wasn't home. I had a moment of fantasy when I expected to see a gray-blue sports car parked there. My mind was not operating in an orderly fashion.

My mother was sitting and waiting for me in the kitchen. She was reading a book at the kitchen table. I had forgotten how much she liked to read.

"Hi," I said. I put down my books.

"Hi," she said. "Want to talk?"

I sat down opposite her. That was my answer.

"So," she said, "how do you feel about your father and me? About everything being permanent?"

"I'm glad for both of you."

"But you're happier for your father than for me, aren't you? I'm still the outsider, aren't I?"

"No. I'm used to your being back. You're my mother. While you were away, you were still my mother. I guess you're wondering how I could be so rotten to my mother. I mean, the accusations about Uncle Mike. How come you didn't bring that up first? Isn't that what's on your mind?"

My mother sighed. "Frankly, if I hear Uncle Mike's stupid name once more, I'll scream. Look, Jody, I had to expect some distrust from you. It happened to surface through Uncle Mike. Now let's get back to your saying that I'm your mother, that you're used to my being back."

"I am. I still don't get this finding-yourself business and you'll probably never make any progress in explaining it to me. I don't see that you've changed at all. But if *you* think you have, and if you're home for good, that's what counts."

"I'm home for good," my mother said.

This seemed like a good occasion to hug each other, but we didn't. We just sat there, contented, the turmoil over.

26

It was the weekend. The first weekend my family had been really together, heart and soul, in over two years. My mother, father, and I were now the real family we appeared to be on Thanksgiving Day.

It was time to think about myself. I went to the telephone and dialed a number. Be home, be home.

"Hello."

"Hi, Matt. It's me."

"Jody?"

"Who else. Want to come by and take some family pictures? My mother, my father, me."

"Is this a test?"

"I guess so."

"I'll take the pictures."

"Understand, I have to know whether you can really accept the Kline family."

"I'd be an idiot not to. *My* parents are back together. My mother, by the way, is now claiming that she never would have married your father."

"Do you believe her?"

"Hard to say. She got the idea from her astrologer."

"Scorpio strikes again."

"She's not Scorpio, and I'm coming over. I'll get some film for my camera and I'll be on my way."

"Forget the camera. I was only testing you."

"But I'd like to take some pictures of *us*. I didn't get any last time. Why don't we go to a park? There's bound to be someone in a park who could take our picture."

Yes indeed, I thought. Someone with a great eye for composition. Someone who could really capture two people in love. I nominate artistic entrepreneur Travis Cameo.

"Jody, are you still there? Don't you want to go to a park?"

"Pictures in the park is a terrific idea. Wear your brown sweater."

"Why?"

"I like it."

"I'll have to wear a jacket over it. It's winter now."

"You're right. We're into our third season. See you soon."

After I hung up, I made another telephone call. It was expensive, but I didn't care. I dialed Opal's number in Montana.

She answered. That is, her voice on an answering machine answered. "Hello to whomever is calling me. If you are a stranger, calling in the hope that I am not home and therefore my house is unoccupied and easy pickings, please be advised that I have a guard dog, one of Montana's finest, in residence. If you are calling legitimately, please leave your name and number at the sound of the beep. Don't be self-conscious and hang up. Do you know how annoying that is?" *Beep!*

The beep came so fast after Opal's message that I wasted a couple of long-distance moments trying to think of the message to leave. Then I said, "Opal, this is Jody. You want news? My mother and father are together again. Matt and I are together again. I'll write you all about—" I got cut off at *about*.

Matt arrived while I was changing my clothes. I pulled my sweater over my head and ran downstairs. My hair must have looked wild. But I didn't want my mother or father to answer the door. I hadn't seen Matt in weeks. Opening the door to Matt was part of our big reunion. I opened the door. It was so incredible and wonderful to see him there again. I guess my parents thought so too, because they came up and stood directly behind me. Matt saw the three of us at the same time.